OF TIME AND CHANCE

Of Time and Chance

A Love Story of the '60s

RUTH PORTER

BAR NOTHING BOOKS

Adamant, Vermont

Published in the United States by
Bar Nothing Books
351 Toby Hill Road
Adamant, VT 05640
802 229-0691
info@barnothingbooks.com
publishing@barnothingbooks.com
SAN 256-615X

Design: Glenn Suokko
Typeset: Adobe Garamond
Printed in the United States

978-1-7378816-0-5 (softback)
978-1-7378816-1-2 (digital)

First Edition

Library of Congress Control Number: 2023901341

Again I saw that under the sun the race is not to the swift, nor the battle to the strong, nor bread to the wise, nor riches to the intelligent, nor favor to the men of skill; but time and chance happen to them all. For man does not know his time. Like fish which are taken in an evil net, and like birds which are caught in a snare, so the sons of men are snared at an evil time, when it suddenly falls upon them.

—Ecclesiastes 9:11–12

CHAPTER I

West Severance, Vermont
June 5, 1967

Andy

When he turned around, the most beautiful girl he had ever seen was standing in the doorway looking at him. Could she be real? She had to be some magic trick of the evening sun, which drew a red-gold line of light around her. Her face was in shadow, but he was positive it would be beautiful too. She was saying something he couldn't understand. It was a blur. He couldn't look and listen at the same time.

He stood there staring at her, holding the milking stool in his hand, while behind him Rosie rattled her stanchion. She wanted to get out to the night pasture with the other cows. He put the pail of milk where it wouldn't get kicked over and let Rosie out. He had to follow her through the barn, so he could open the gate for her, and he knew when he got back to the milk room, the beautiful vision would be gone.

But he was wrong. She was there, and she was smiling. She said, "Can I buy your milk? My sister and I came to buy milk from your farm, and there it is, plenty of it. How much do you want for the whole pail full?"

He stood there in confusion, and worse, he could feel the red flush climbing up his cheeks to embarrass him. He said, "The milk you want is up at the house. It's already bottled for you."

"But I want your milk."

He didn't know what to say to that, and he could feel his face getting redder. He just stood there, looking at her.

"Okay, what about this then? Will you teach me how to milk?"

She was even more beautiful when she smiled, and she was smiling at *him*, but before he could think of a reply, someone called from up near the house, and the girl turned and left.

He went to the door. She was just hurrying around the corner of the barn. She didn't look back.

He spent a little while straightening up the milk room, trying to calm down. He put a dish of fresh milk out for the barn cats. He should have offered her the pail of milk. He should have said he would teach her how to milk. He could have put Rosie back in the stanchion. He might have been able to squeeze a few more squirts of milk out of her, while he and the girl sat there close together. But it was too late. And maybe she was just joking. With her long flowing hair and long flowing skirt, she didn't look like someone who wanted to learn how to milk.

Anyway, it was over. He sighed and picked up the pail. When he got around the corner of the barn, he saw there were no cars parked in front, so she was truly gone.

Just then Gram came around the outside of the house. "Where's your Ma at, Andy? I heard her callin. I was out back in the garden."

"Ma's car ain't here. She could be pickin Phyllis up from school. Maybe they went downstreet or somethin."

"Well, I better get supper goin. I want to make some hamburgs out of that new meat."

"Make a lot of 'em. I'm hungry."

"You always are, and I always do."

They went into the house together. Andy kicked off his boots and took the milk to the back room and put it through the strainer. He washed the milk pail in the sink and set it out on the counter to dry. "If you don't need me to do nothin, Gram, I got some homework."

"You go do that, honey. I don't need any help."

Upstairs in his room, Andy changed his shirt and pants. He hung the clothes that smelled like cow on the back of his door to air out. He got his big American History book and lay down on his bed to read the assignment. They were getting close to the end of the school year and close to the end of the book. Gram was probably alive for most of what he had to read. He wished she could just tell him how it was, so he didn't have to read it. If she told it, it might even stay in his head.

He tried to picture Gram as a young girl and that led him right into thinking about the beautiful girl in the barn. She was dressed like a hippie. There were girls in his class who tried to dress that way, but none of them looked like she did. She must have been from down-country some place. She was just passing through, and he would never see her again.

He lay on his bed with the big book making a comfortable weight on his stomach while he thought about her. He was planning to start reading, when Pop shouted to him to come to supper. He closed the book and hurried downstairs.

Everyone was at the table when he got there. He slid into his chair and reached for the food. They were all eating already. For a little while, he had forgotten how hungry he was.

At first, everyone was too busy to make conversation. After a while, Phyllis said, "I saw Bobby Jacobs in the grocery store, and he said to say hi to you, Andy."

"Okay."

"He said to tell you they're all goin to the recruitin office on graduation day."

"Everybody knows that already, Phyllis."

"What?" Pop said. "What's that about?"

"A whole bunch of the guys in my class are goin to join the army after graduation. That's all."

"Oh," Pop said. "I thought it was like a protest or somethin. Are you goin with 'em, Andy?"

Andy sighed. "I want to, but I can't, not unless you and Ma sign for me. I've told you that before."

"I guess I forgot. Well, I'll do it. I don't want to hold you up, if that's what you want to do."

"Thanks, Pop."

"Patty, is it okay with you if I sign, so Andy can join the army?"

Everybody looked at Ma, but she didn't say anything.

Andy said, "It ain't a big deal, Ma. When my birthday gets here, and I'm eighteen, I can sign for myself. We're just talkin about a couple months, so I can go when my friends go."

She didn't even answer. She just threw down her fork and ran out of the room, leaving the rest of them looking at each other.

Phyllis said, "You could sign for Andy, Pop, even if she doesn't want to."

"I ain't goin to do that. I'll talk to her about it. I can bring her around. I know that's what you want, Andy."

Andy nodded. "Thanks, Pop."

Cynthia

She held Orion on her lap while Laura drove. They were going to buy some milk at a farm Laura knew about. She had to joggle Orion up and down to keep him from crying. It worked until the car stopped.

Laura got out and came around to the passenger side. "Here. I'll take him. I'm going to have to feed him before I show you how we buy milk here. It won't take long." She took the baby and got in the back seat. When she began to unbutton her blouse, he stopped crying.

Cynthia got out of the car. They were parked in front of an old farmhouse that once had been painted white. There was a barn attached to one end of it. She said, "I don't think anyone's home."

"That doesn't matter. I'll show you in a minute."

"Okay. Call me when Orion's done. I'm going to explore." She walked along the barn wall. Around the corner, the evening light shone with a golden haze on the old red of the barn boards. There was an open door. She stopped and looked in.

It took a minute for her eyes to adjust to the dusty darkness in the room. Then she saw that a cow was standing there, and a man was sitting under the cow with his back to the door. He was milking. Cynthia could hear the staccato bursts of milk hitting the side of the metal bucket.

The cow shifted her feet and turned her head, rolling her bulging eyeballs around to see who was standing in the door.

The man reached up and smacked her on the flank. "Quit it, Rosie. What's got into you anyhow?" He started to milk again.

It was like watching a movie, but better, because she was in it too. She could smell the milk and the manure and the animal smell of the cow. She could feel the warm spring sun on her back. It was another world, one she had only read about in books.

The man said, "Okay, Rosie. You're all done." He stood up and stretched. When he reached down for the stool, he turned, and that was when he saw Cynthia standing in the doorway.

She saw that he wasn't a man, at all. He was a boy, and he was about her age. He stood there, not saying anything, just looking at her.

The cow shook her head, rattling the bars that held her. The boy put down the stool and moved the milk pail out of the way. Then he opened the bar around the cow's neck, and she stepped daintily out and walked through a door into another part of the barn. The boy followed her.

Cynthia wanted to see where they went, but the floor was mucky, and her feet were bare. She thought about how she could take the pail and carry it to the car. She would say, "I got us some milk, Laura. Do you think this will be enough?" She was laughing to herself about how surprised Laura would be, when the boy came back.

Still in the spirit of the joke, she said, "My sister and I came to your farm to buy some milk. How much do you want for what's in that pail? I can get the money from my sister."

For some reason, that made the boy blush. He mumbled something about getting milk at the house.

She didn't know what he meant. "Well, okay," she said. "If you won't sell us any, will you teach me to milk? I've always wanted to know how." That wasn't strictly true, but the smile she turned on him was, and that made up for it.

She was about to say more. It was tempting to try to darken the flush on his face, but just then she heard Laura calling her. She sounded impatient. Cynthia hurried out the door and around the corner of the barn.

Laura was standing beside her car with Orion on her hip. There was a big jar of milk and a carton of eggs sitting on the roof of the car. As soon as she saw Cynthia, she said, "Where were you? I wanted to show you how to buy milk here."

"There was a boy milking a cow in the barn. I was watching him."

"Here. Take Orion. We need to get home."

"What's the hurry? I thought you were going to show me around."

"It's getting late, and I don't need to show it to you. It's easy. There's a refrigerator on the porch. You take what you want and leave the money. It's all marked. There's even a dish of change in case you need it."

They got into the car. "Aren't they afraid people will take milk without paying for it? Or maybe take money?"

"They trust people. They've been doing it this way for a long time, I think. I guess it works."

"That boy in the barn told me he would teach me how to milk. He was cute."

Laura looked around in surprise, but she didn't say anything.

"I think I'll take him up on it."

When they were driving up the hill to Laura's house, Cynthia remembered what she had forgotten to tell Laura. "Mom said she and Dad are going to come up to visit in a few weeks."

"What?"

"I meant to tell you yesterday when I got here, but I forgot."

"When, Cynthy? I'm going to have to get ready for them. They might not like it that we're letting a lot of people live here."

"Who's living here besides us? Just Bob Wickelow, right? He's the only person I met last night."

"People come and go. We try not to turn our friends away if they need a place to stay for a while. Everyone's moving around a lot these days, especially people in the counterculture."

"I like that, Laura, but while Mom and Dad are visiting, maybe it's not such a good idea. They are so old-fashioned."

Laura parked beside Cynthia's little Volkswagen beetle. Paul's old pickup was on the other side of Cynthia's car. "Oh look, Paul's home already. I need to get going on supper."

"I'll help you. I want to learn how to cook." They got out of the car. "There are so many things I want to learn how to do." But she was really talking to herself, because Laura had taken Orion and was hurrying into the house to see Paul.

After supper, Cynthia helped Laura with the dishes, while Paul sat on the porch holding Orion and listening to Bob Wickelow playing his guitar and singing, "Where Have all the Flowers Gone?"

They left the door open so they could hear him while they straightened up the kitchen. There was only a thin line of light along the horizon when they finished and went out onto the porch. It was dark, except for the light coming through the windows and the screen door. Paul sat in the shadows, cradling Orion in his arms.

Laura stopped by Paul's chair. She bent down and kissed Orion on the head. He didn't move. She took off her sweater and laid it over him like a blanket. Then she sat down on the porch steps.

Cynthia sat down beside her. There was a sliver of moon. The brightest stars were just beginning to appear. Cynthia wrapped her skirts around her legs. The night air was cold. Bob was singing "Blowin in the Wind," one of her favorite songs. It reminded her of the big protest in New York in April, her first real antiwar protest.

The air smelled of cedar and ice water. Laura must be even colder without her sweater. Cynthia thought that when the song was over, she would go inside and get a blanket for them to share, but before Bob got to the last verse, the phone rang. Laura jumped up and went inside to answer it. Cynthia tried to listen, but she couldn't hear much because Bob was still singing and playing his guitar.

After a while, Laura came back. She stood in the doorway, silhouetted by the light from the kitchen. She waited until Bob got to the end of the song, and then she said, "That was Mom on the phone. She and Dad would like to come up and see us the weekend after next."

Bob played a chord on his guitar.

Cynthia said, "Didn't she want to talk to me?"

"She sent her love and said she'd see you soon. Is that okay with you, Paul? Cynthia told me about it this afternoon, but I didn't get a chance to ask you."

"It's fine with me. They haven't been up since last fall when Orion was born. I'm sure they want to see him."

Orion heard their voices and woke up, adding his fretful comments to the conversation.

"Here, Paul. Let me have him. I'll feed him, so we can put him down for the night."

Paul stood, and she sat down in the chair and took the baby. Paul carefully wrapped her sweater around her shoulders. She looked up and smiled at him.

Cynthia watched the whole exchange, trying not to feel jealous. She wished there was someone who felt so tenderly protective of her.

Bob said, "Why don't I get out of your way when they come? I've been thinking about going home for a visit before I head out west this summer."

Laura looked up at Bob. "That's a good idea. Thanks. It would make things less complicated."

Nellie

At first, everyone was too hungry to talk, but later in the meal, Phyllis and Andy started talking about how all Andy's friends were joining the army after graduation, and how Andy couldn't go with them because he wasn't eighteen yet. Frank said he would sign for him, but that upset Patty so much that she ran out of the room and didn't come back.

After supper, Frank went to watch the television news, and Andy went back to his homework. Nellie got up to clear the table.

"I can help you clean up, Gram," Phyllis said.

"What about your homework?"

"It's okay. I ain't got much tonight."

So Nellie brought the dirty dishes over to the sink and put away the food, while Phyllis washed.

"It ain't but a couple of weeks until Andy's graduation. What're you goin to wear, Gram?"

"I don't know. I'll find somethin. Who's goin to look at a old lady anyway?"

Phyllis hugged her with dripping hands. "Oh Gram, I want you to look beautiful."

"Thank you, honey. But you're gettin me all wet. What about you? What are you goin to wear?"

"I'm sorry I dripped on you." She took the dish towel and wiped at Nellie's shoulders and back. "I don't know what to wear. I ain't got nothin good enough."

"What about that blue skirt your ma bought you with the pink flowers on it? You look pretty in that."

"It's too long. It looks funny. Nobody I know wears 'em long like that. I wanted Ma to put up the hem, but she ain't got time."

"I can do it for you."

"Oh Gram, really?"

"Sure. It won't take long. You'll have to put it on, so I can see what to do."

When they were all done in the kitchen, Phyllis went upstairs to get the skirt, while Nellie got her box of pins and her reading glasses. She took the salt and pepper and sugar off the kitchen table.

When Phyllis came back, Nellie told her to get up on the table.

"What?" Phyllis looked horrified. "You want me to stand on the table? Where we eat?"

"I have to be able to see the bottom of your skirt to pin it."

"But I'll get the table all dirty."

"Take off your shoes and socks."

"Really, Gram?"

"Really. We'll wash it off after. I got to be able to see to pin your hem, and I'm too old to be crouchin down on the floor."

Phyllis climbed up on the table barefoot and stood there, turning slowly, while Nellie pinned the hem. She was about halfway around when Frank came in.

"Where's…Phyllis, what're you doin up there?"

"Gram's fixin my skirt for me."

"But that's where we eat."

"We'll wash it off when we're done, Pop."

"You better do a good job. Our food goes on that table." He looked at Nellie. "Where's Patty, Ma?"

Nellie had to take the pins out of her mouth to answer. "Have you looked upstairs? She didn't come back down."

"Okay. I'll go look."

When Nellie had the skirt pinned all the way around, she took off her close-work glasses and stood back. "I like it," she said. Phyllis looked sweet and pretty, not like her usual tomboy self.

"You can get down. And give me the skirt. I've got a little time tonight. I can start on it."

"But if I take off the skirt, I'll be in my underpants."

"That's okay. There ain't nobody around. Give me the skirt."

Phyllis took it off and scurried upstairs. Nellie wiped the table and put the salt and pepper and sugar back in the middle of it. She took the skirt and went to the front room to sit down with her sewing basket.

The window was open, and mist was rolling up from the valley. The outside air came in, full of earthy smells. There was ice in it too, but the spring peepers were singing a song of the new season and their hopes for it.

She got about halfway around the skirt before she had to quit. Her eyes wouldn't focus any more. Even with her glasses jammed on tight, her eyes jumped all over the place when she tried to see her stitches. She turned out the light and went up to bed. The house was silent. There was a crack of light under Andy's door. She went on by. She could finish the hem tomorrow. Phyllis wouldn't need it until the end of next week.

CHAPTER 2

After school, when Andy went outside, he saw some of his friends gathered around one of the benches. He joined them. It was a sunny afternoon. Everyone was joking around, giving Dougie a hard time because he said he wasn't going to the prom.

Rickie must have noticed that Andy wasn't joining in, because all of a sudden he said, "Well, what about you, Keyes? I bet you're bringin old Sandra Banks, right?"

"No, I ain't."

Why not?"

"I don't like her no more, that's why."

"What's the matter? You wasn't gettin any?"

Andy shrugged.

"If you took her to the prom, she might…"

"Well, I'm not takin her. Besides, I ain't got a suit that fits me."

"What're you goin to do about graduation?"

"My old one won't show. The robe'll be over it."

Rickie said, "Hey guys, guess what? Andy ain't got a date either."

Somebody said, "You ought to ask Dougie to be your date."

Everyone laughed at that, and Andy and Dougie tried to act like they thought it was funny too.

After that, they started to talk about meeting up as soon as they got their diplomas, so they could all go down to the recruiting office together. Andy looked for a chance to get away without anybody noticing. He didn't want to have to say that he wasn't going with them. He thought he'd take his diploma and leave with his family. He could go home and change into his work clothes and clean the barn or something. He was still going to have to get through the whole summer before he could join up with the guys.

A few days later, he hitched into town to see if he could find a job. He really didn't care what it was. All he wanted was something to pass the time until he could enlist and go to Vietnam with everybody else.

He spent the whole day looking. A few places told him to check back in a week or two, but that was it.

On the edge of town, he stuck out his thumb for a ride. Two cars passed without slowing down. Then a little black Volkswagen with Connecticut plates went by. He kept his thumb out, even though he knew flatlanders hardly ever picked up hitchhikers and certainly not local ones.

The Volkswagen slowed down and stopped on the edge of the road about twenty feet away. He didn't think it was waiting for him, but he walked up to it and opened the door to ask. He had to bend way down to see the driver.

He couldn't believe his eyes. It was the beautiful girl who came to the farm to buy milk a few weeks ago. He had thought about her a lot, but he never thought he would see her again. He could feel the blood going up his face. "Did you stop to give me a ride?

"Well, of course. Get in."

He did. It wasn't easy to fit his long legs under the dashboard. She sped off, and for a minute neither of them spoke.

Then he said, "Thanks for pickin me up, but you really shouldn't pick up strangers. It's dangerous."

"I didn't."

"What?"

"I didn't pick up a stranger. I recognized you."

He couldn't think clearly while she was smiling at him.

"You're the guy from the Keyes farm where my sister buys milk. Is that where you're going now?"

"Yeah, but you don't have to..."

"That's okay. I have to go almost to your road to get to my sister's."

"Your sister's?" He wanted to ask if she was living with her sister, but he didn't know how to say it.

"She and her husband have a farmhouse on a hill, kind of like yours. They bought it last year. I think it's called the Robinson Farm."

"That's your sister's? I know that place. They turned it into a commune."

She looked around at him. "Is that what people say about it?"

"Some people, I guess."

"It's not a commune. It's just that a lot of their friends stay with them."

He didn't say anything, but she seemed to read his mind.

"I've been staying with them too. I love it there. I think I'll stay for a while." She smiled right at him. "So, you see, you'll have time to teach me how to milk."

"Our woodlot backs up on the Robinson woodlot."

"Are you serious?"

"I used to hunt over there."

"Will you show me?"

"I might could…"

"Now there are two things I want you to show me, because I still want to learn how to milk. Are you planning to teach me that?"

"I hadn't planned…but I could." It was a lot to take in, and they were getting close to his road. "You can let me off at the bottom of the hill," he said.

"Are you sure? I don't mind taking you up to the house."

"This is better. If they see you, they'll ask a lot of questions." He didn't want Phyllis to see her.

"Okay. Have it your way." She stopped the car. "But you have to tell me your name."

"It's Andy." He got out of the car and leaned down to look in at her. "What's yours?"

"Crystal," she said.

"That's beautiful." He was thinking about how it suited her. "Like a star," he said. And then he had to shut the door quickly, as she put the car in gear.

She wheeled around, and as she left, she looked at him through the open window. "I'll be seeing you, Andy Keyes." She drove off with a roar. Something was going on with her engine. He could hear it and smell it. She might let him fix it for her, although it probably would cost more than he could come up with.

At least he knew her name and that she wanted to see him again. The wind picked up as he was walking up the hill. There was going to be a thunderstorm before long.

When he brought the milk in the house, Gram asked him if he found a job. He said he hadn't had much luck, and she was surprised. She said he looked so happy that she thought he must have found a good one. He didn't say anything. He didn't want to explain why he was feeling so pleased.

After supper he was in the shed when Phyllis showed up. She stood right in the door, blocking the light.

"What're you doin out here, Andy?"

"Gettin some tools. Move out of the way. I'm in a hurry."

"What for?"

"It'll be dark pretty soon. I'm makin a trail up in the woods."

"For huntin?"

"Maybe." He had an ax and a buck saw. That would be enough for tonight. The ax needed sharpening, but he decided not to bother.

"Can I come with you?"

"No, you can't."

"I won't get in the way, Andy. I could carry your tools for you."

"You'd talk. I want to be by myself."

"I won't say a word, Andy. I promise."

"The answer is still no, Phyllis. Now get out of the way. I'll be back when it gets too dark to work any more."

She stepped aside, and he went out the door. She followed him.

"You were gone all day. Where'd you go?"

"Downstreet lookin for a job."

"Did you get one?"

"No."

She followed him up to the pasture gate. "How'd you get there, anyhow?"

"I hitched. That's how."

"I could do that."

"Don't you try it. Fourteen's too young, and anyway, it's different for a girl."

"Boys have all the luck."

"Girls don't get drafted. You luck out that way."

"I thought you wanted to go to the army."

"I do. But it wouldn't matter if I didn't. I'd get drafted anyway."

"You mean you wouldn't go if you didn't have to?"

"Come on, Phyl. Our country's at war. Of course, I want to go. Now get down to the house, because you can't come with me."

He walked away up the pasture. The grass was wet from the storm, but the sky was clear again. There was already one star shining. He could feel Phyllis watching him walk away. When he got almost to the top of the field, he looked down toward the gate, but no one was there.

He turned and went into the trees. Last year they cut firewood down below the house, so there were a lot of low bushes and weeds on the logging road. He could see where it went up the hill, but he wanted it to be clear even to someone who didn't know much about the woods. He set the saw down on the edge of the road and started chopping the bushes off at ground level. He was glad he hadn't bothered to sharpen the ax, since he kept hitting stones under the ground.

When he stopped for a breather, he noticed the quiet. It was that time just before night when everything is still. The only sound was the occasional tick of a raindrop falling from a tree onto the leaves below. Beyond the black lines of the tree trunks, the light in the field was as clear as water.

He had worked a short distance up the hill when he heard an animal walking through the leaves. After a minute it stopped. He thought it might be a squirrel running between trees, and he went back to work, but the next time he stopped, he heard it again. It was off to the east and downhill of where he was chopping.

He pretended to go to work again, but he was really watching, and this time he saw a silhouette moving from one tree to another against the fading light from the field. For a second he was afraid, but just for a second.

"Phyllis, I know that's you."

There was nothing for a minute, and then she stepped out from behind a tree. "Don't be mad, Andy. I just wanted to see what you were doin."

"I already *told* you what I was doin. Go on down."

"But, Andy, I could help. You used to let me help you. I'm even bigger and stronger than I used to be. So why can't I help?"

"You just can't. That's why. And you shouldn't sneak up on people in the woods. It ain't safe. I could have a gun with me."

"There's all summer till huntin season."

He sighed and picked up the saw and started down the hill to the house. Phyllis trailed behind him.

Neither of them said anything. As they walked, the sweet smell of the wet grass came up to him mixed with the spicy night air, filling his heart with longing.

CHAPTER 3

Cynthia and Laura were sitting at the kitchen table drinking coffee, while Laura fed Orion some solid food. It was cereal, and he didn't like it. He was sitting in his highchair with a bib around his neck. Some of the time when Laura held out a spoonful, he would open his mouth for it, but then he would make a face and push it out. Laura would have to scrape it off his chin and give it to him again. It was very slow.

They were talking about Mom and Dad's visit. Laura said there was a lot to do to get ready.

Cynthia said, "I thought I would wash the windows."

"That's a big job."

"We've got almost a week. I ought to be able to get the downstairs ones done at least. Remember how Mom used to get after us when we put our fingers on the glass?"

Laura laughed. Orion thought she was laughing at him. He blew a mouthful of cereal out. Maybe he thought it would make her laugh even harder, but Laura scolded him, and his face crumpled up. He was just about to cry.

Bob Wickelow walked into the room carrying an armful of clothes. He stopped by the table. "Hey, little buddy," he said to Orion. "Why the sad face?" Then to Laura, he said, "I'm cleaning out my stuff. You can use the room if you want to."

"You don't need to bother. We're going to fix Cynthia's room for Mom and Dad. It's bigger."

"I need to do it anyway. I want to take a load of stuff home before I go out west."

"Thanks, Bob."

"I'm coming back after the weekend. I'm planning to leave from here, if that's okay. I have to have some work done on my car before I head out."

It was Friday. Cynthia and Laura were talking about Mom and Dad's visit, which was going to happen tomorrow. Paul was with them on the porch, holding Orion on his lap. Cynthia sat on the steps, looking out at the night.

Laura said, "They probably won't get here until sometime in the afternoon. It takes almost five hours from Stamford."

Cynthia looked up into the sky, which wasn't really black if you looked closely. It was a deep, deep blue with the stars spangled across it. She said, "I hope it's good weather when they're here. They're going to love this view. It's so peaceful and quiet."

Just then there was the sound of a car without a muffler roaring in the distance. They all laughed. Orion sat straighter, looking out toward the noise. Paul jiggled him up and down to keep him from being afraid. The sound kept getting louder, and soon it was obvious that the car was coming up their hill.

"Who could it be, Paul?" Laura said.

"I don't know, but we're just about to find out."

The car came around the last curve and roared up to the house in a swirl of exhaust fumes. They watched as two women got out.

Paul said, "I'm glad it's not Bob. I thought he might be coming back with car trouble."

The women stopped at the bottom of the steps. The one in front said, "Remember me, Laura? Gail Levine? We were in biology class together."

"Oh sure, I remember. It's been a while. How are you?"

"I'm all right, but I need a favor. This is my friend, Angela. She wasn't in college when you and Paul were there."

Cynthia was watching Angela. She stayed a few steps behind her friend and said nothing.

"Come up on the porch and sit down. Paul, give me Orion, and get them some chairs."

"Ooh, you have a baby now. Is it a boy? He's so cute. I remember when you guys got married." Gail turned toward Angela. "They had the ceremony in the woods behind the school. It was in the spring. It was very romantic."

"Our mom and dad didn't think so. They thought we should have the wedding in a church."

Cynthia moved over on the steps, so they could walk up. She said, "They always think we don't know what we're doing, but they come around eventually."

"We don't want to put you out, but everybody on campus talks about how generous you guys are about letting people stay with you when they need a place."

Laura said, "That was Paul's idea. I remember when we decided to buy this farm, we agreed that we wanted to share it. He convinced me it was the best way to do it."

When they were sitting down and had all been introduced to each other, Gail said, "It's such a beautiful night."

"Cynthia and I were just saying how we hoped this weather would last through the weekend. Our parents are coming up for a visit tomorrow."

"And we were just about to ask you if we could stay with you. Angela, here, is in trouble, and it's my fault. We need a place to hide out for a few days."

Cynthia sat there wondering why Laura hadn't seen this coming. She might have headed it off if she had. But Laura just asked what the trouble was.

"It's her boyfriend. He's a really bad guy. I've been trying to get her to leave him for a while now, but she has been too scared to do it. Tonight I was at their place when he went out to get a six-pack, and I talked her into making a run for it. He might come after both of us now, and he might recognize my car. It was parked right out in front of their apartment."

"That's awful," Laura said. "Do you really think he might come after you?"

"What do you think, Angela?"

"That's what he always says he'll do if I try to leave him."

Paul hadn't said anything until now. "Does he have a gun?"

Everyone looked at Angela.

"Well, yeah, he has a lot of hunting equipment."

Laura sighed. "I think you'd better stay here tonight. Suppose he's driving around looking for you. I mean, your car is kind of noticeable."

Everyone laughed.

"But tomorrow you'll have to find another place to hide, because of Mom and Dad coming."

"We can do that. Thanks, Laura."

Paul helped them put the car out of sight behind the house. Cynthia went with Laura to fix up Bob's room. Laura sat in a chair feeding Orion while Cynthia put clean sheets on the bed. It wasn't a double bed, but they would have to manage.

"I was surprised when you said they could stay. I was waiting for you to tell them they couldn't."

"Oh, I know. I was planning to tell them that. It was the gun that did it. I have so much trouble sticking up for myself. I wish I could learn better."

"It's nice of you, Laura. You're so generous. I would have told them no way. They'll have to leave in the morning, but I can help you with that."

"Thanks, Cynthy. I don't know why I have so much trouble saying no when someone asks me for a favor. As soon as she asked me, I got into a panic, wondering how I could say no, and that talk about a gun put me over the edge. It's not my problem. I don't know Angela at all, and I hardly know Gail. I wouldn't have even recognized her if she hadn't said who she was."

"We'll fix it in the morning. Do you think I need to give them another blanket?'

"It's a warm night. They'll be fine." She stood up. "Look at Orion. He's limp. I'd better see if I can put him down without waking him. You could show them where they can sleep."

"Okay. And Laura, I meant it when I said I'd help you get them to leave in the morning."

"Thanks, Cynthy." She left the room carrying Orion, and Cynthia went downstairs.

The next afternoon, Cynthia was on the porch, waiting for Mom and

Dad while she watched Orion crawl around the floor. She had spread out a blanket so he wouldn't get dirty. They had had a busy morning doing last minute things to get ready after Gail and Angela left.

When she saw their car coming up the hill, she picked up Orion and the blanket. Mom might not approve of her putting him down on the floor. She went over to the car as they were getting out.

"Oh, let me hold that baby. He's so big. I don't believe it. It has been too long."

Cynthia kissed Mom hello and handed Orion to her. She went around the car, "Hello Dad. Give me something to carry. I'll show you where to put your things."

They all went into the kitchen together. When Orion saw Laura, he started to wiggle out of Mom's arms. He had been suspicious of her cooing over him, and when he saw his mother, he realized where he wanted to be.

Laura wiped her floury hands on her apron. "Here, Mom, I'll take him. Did you have a good trip?"

Dad said, "It was easy, except that we had to stop at Basketville. That took some time."

"Well, of course we had to stop. We might have found some baskets for Laura's house. We didn't, but we could have."

Cynthia showed them where to put their suitcases and came back to the kitchen to take Orion, so Laura could go back to cooking. Orion accepted the transfer. He seemed to think the invasion was over.

Later, at dinner, Dad asked Paul what he thought about Cassius Clay refusing to sign up for induction into the army. "Don't you think they ought to find him guilty?"

"He says he's a conscientious objector and that his religion thinks this war is wrong."

"What kind of religion is it anyway? He's a public figure, and he pulls this stunt just when we're finally turning the corner on the war. It's disgraceful."

"He has a right to try for CO status if he thinks the war is a mistake."

"That's naïve. If we don't all stand together, the communists will take over all of Vietnam, and then what? It's on the television news every night. You must see it."

"I read a lot of newspapers. We don't have a television."

"You don't? Maybe that's what's wrong. If you had a television, you would see how important it is that we all support our government."

Mom said, "I thought we agreed that we weren't going to talk politics on this visit."

Paul didn't say anything, and Laura jumped in to change the subject.

In the late afternoon on Sunday, Cynthia offered to go get some milk and eggs. "I'll bring Mom and show her how we buy stuff from the Keyes farm. She'll like it."

On the way, they talked about the visit. Mom said they had to head home tomorrow, but before they left, Dad wanted to go into town to buy Laura and Paul a television set.

"You don't need to do that. They'll buy one if they want one."

"They need to be aware of what's happening in the world."

"Everyone is already. Everyone has an opinion about Vietnam. It's just that we have different ideas than you do."

"That's why we need to get a television."

Cynthia sighed. There wasn't any use in arguing with people over thirty, even if they were your own family. "I hope they'll be able to get reception. They'll have to put up an antenna and hook it up somehow."

"We won't be able to do that. We have to get home before dark."

When they got to the Keyes farm, Cynthia stopped in front of the house and turned off the car. No one was around.

"Cynthia, what are you doing?"

"This is where Laura buys her milk, Mom. Come on. I want to show you. I didn't believe it at first. It's such a neat system."

On the porch, Cynthia took two half-gallon jars of milk and a dozen blue eggs. She left the money on the table. Mom didn't say anything, but Cynthia could tell she was watching.

She wanted to go around the corner of the barn to see if Andy

Keyes was there, but she couldn't leave Mom, and she didn't want to bring her.

On the way home, she said she thought it was great that the Keyes trusted their customers the way they did.

Mom said, "Do you think that milk is pasteurized?"

"I don't know."

"Well, that's not okay. It's dangerous to drink raw milk. Laura must not do that. There are lots of diseases you can get. What about brucellosis?"

Cynthia sighed again. "You need to talk to Laura about that."

"I'm going to. She shouldn't take chances with Orion's health."

Neither of them spoke after that. Cynthia had been planning to point out the beauty of the countryside, but she lost heart and drove straight back to Laura's.

CHAPTER 4

Nellie decided she would finish the row of potatoes she was working on in the garden before she stopped. It was late morning. The sun was shining, and it was already hot. There were four more rows to hill, but it was still early days. The potatoes wouldn't flower for another week or two.

While she hoed, she thought about Andy's graduation last week. It was quite an event, although Andy didn't win any prizes or get special mention. But it was very rare that the whole family went anyplace together. That made it special. Nellie was surprised that Andy didn't want to stay with his friends instead of coming straight home with the family, but other than that, it all went well and was good to think about.

The screen door slammed, and Nellie looked at the house. Phyllis was walking toward the garden. She was eating something. Nellie stopped working and stood for a minute, leaning on the hoe.

Phyllis came closer. She was eating a slice of bread with so much jam that globs of it dripped off as she walked. Nellie could just picture the kitchen counter.

"You missed breakfast. I hope you didn't leave a mess in the kitchen."

"I didn't, Gram." She got to the edge of the garden and stopped, looking down. "Uh-oh, Gram, what's this here?"

Nellie went over to see. It was a small, clear footprint of a deer in the soft earth. They looked around. There were several more footprints, but nothing had been eaten.

"Not yet, anyway," Nellie said. "There'll be more damage soon. So far she's just checkin things out."

"Pop could shoot her for you, Gram."

"I could do it myself. I'm a better shot than he is."

"You ought to teach me, Gram. You taught Andy, and you taught Pop. Now it's my turn."

"I will, honey."

"I want to be a real good shot, like you."

"It takes practice, but there's plenty of places to practice around here. I'll show you a few things on the deer rifle. Then you can get some practice protectin the garden." She picked up the hoe and went back to hilling the potatoes.

"I can help you now. You'll get through sooner, and you'll have more time to give me a lesson."

"I'm almost done here, but I have some laundry to put out on the line. You can help with that. Right now you need to stand out of the way so I can finish the row."

"Sorry, Gram." She moved a few feet. "We'd better get another dog. The deer didn't come so close before Penny got sick."

"She was a help."

"Do you think Ma and Pop would let me have a dog? I could spend the whole summer trainin it."

"You'll have to ask them."

"You should tell them we really need a dog to protect our garden."

"Both of us should tell them."

"A dog would keep your chickens safe too."

Nellie thought, "Unless the dog went after them himself," but she didn't say it out loud.

After supper when they finished cleaning up, Patty said, "I think Frank's sittin on the porch. Are you comin out?"

"I'll be along in a minute. I want to get some socks to mend."

"I should be mendin somethin too, but it's a beautiful evenin, and I'm tired."

"You go on, Patty. You do enough, workin downstreet all day. I'll join you in a minute."

"Thanks, Nellie."

When she got there, she saw that they had left the rocker for her. She set the sewing basket on the floor beside it and put her glasses on her lap.

They all three sat looking out across the valley. It was very quiet. Once in a while there was a peeper calling, but peepers were pretty much done for the year now, and the crickets hadn't really gotten started. There was a cool breeze from the northwest.

"You did good to cut today, Frank. It feels like a run of hay weather."

"I thought so. I cut both front fields."

"I can smell it."

"There wasn't so much in the one where we put the corn. We ought to be able to get both fields put away." He reached down and rapped his knuckles on the wooden floor. "Barrin breakdowns and if the weather holds."

"Everythin's workin all right, ain't it?"

"I got to grease up the baler and check it out."

"Andy can do that for you."

"If I could catch up with him, he might. Where's he at tonight?"

Phyllis had come around the side of the house and was just sitting down on the steps.

"What do you know about Andy, Phyl?"

"He's probably up in the woods, workin on his trail."

"What's that?"

"He's makin a trail up to the top of the hill."

"What's he doin that for?"

"I don't know," Phyllis said. "He won't tell me what it's about. He just says it's for huntin season, and that don't make any sense, because he ain't even goin to be here in huntin season."

Nellie put down the sock she had just started to fix. "He sure does love the woods. Let him fool around up there if that's what he wants to do. It's probably his way of sayin goodbye to the place. Remember how you fixed everythin before you left for the war, Frank?"

"I ain't botherin him, Gram. I could help him if he'd let me."

"He might could want to be alone, you know."

"Did you tell Pop about the deer?"

"Nobody's told me nothin. What about a deer?"

Nellie said, "We saw hoofprints in the garden. We're goin to have some trouble this year."

"It's because Penny died. Gram and I think we need a new dog. Can we get one, Ma? I could spend the whole summer trainin it."

"I don't know. A dog can be a lot of trouble. Of course, Penny was different. What do you say, Frank?"

"Oh please, Pop, oh, please…"

"Gimme a minute to think, Phyllis."

"Okay, Pop, but we really need a dog."

"What about it, Ma?" Frank said.

"Phyllis says she'll take care of it…"

"Oh, I will, I will!"

"It'll have to stay outside."

"Penny came in when it was cold."

"Well, if you're goin to start that…"

"I won't, Pop. It can stay outside. I won't say no more about it comin in, but please…"

Patty said, "We could go to the shelter and see what they have."

Phyllis was bouncing around on the step in her effort to not say any more.

"I guess you could go look, if your Ma wants to carry you to the shelter."

"Oh goody! When can we go, Ma? Can we go tomorrow?"

"Phyllis, don't nag. We'll go as soon as we can."

Nellie said, "When this batch of hay's in the barn, there'll be time…maybe."

"It's always goin to be somethin…"

Nobody said anything, and Phyllis was wise enough to see that she'd pushed it right up to the limit.

After a while, Nellie said, "A night like this makes me so grateful that we didn't sell out when your dad died. Remember, Frank, how everybody but you thought we ought to move into town?"

"I never wanted to leave."

"I know. You were the only one who thought we ought to stay here."

Patty said, "I can't imagine Frank livin in town."

Nellie said, "My mother and sisters thought he'd have a better chance in town, a better education—all that. I was so stunned by Phil's death that I couldn't think at all. We tried to sell out, but it was the Depression, and no one was buyin."

Frank said, "I was hammered too. It was so sudden. The only thing I knew was that I didn't want to leave."

"Well, it turned out. Didn't it? Your dad would have been proud of us, the way we kept the place goin."

"You did it alone when I was gone to the war."

"It felt like if I could just keep the place up and runnin, you would make it home again." She picked up the sock in her lap and started to darn it. "And that's what happened."

Phyllis wasn't sitting on the stops any more. The old people talking ancient history had driven her away.

After a while, Frank said, "What do you think about a deer in the garden, Ma?"

"We saw tracks, and it's pretty early in the season. A dog might help."

"Not if she comes home with a puppy, but it don't matter. I've been plannin to put a light back there anyhow. I'll get to it soon. Then we can have some of your deer meat stew."

"I gave Phyllis a shootin lesson this afternoon."

Patty said, "But she's a girl. She don't need to know that stuff."

"She asked me to teach her, Patty. If you don't want me to, I won't show her anymore."

"Oh no, I guess it's okay."

Frank said, "Sure. She could turn out to be a good shot like Ma here. Then we'd always have venison on hand. I'll get a floodlight set up, and we'll see what happens."

"Maybe we'll have a dog soon too. It's goin to be a good garden if we can keep the pests out of it."

They were all quiet for a while, and then Frank sighed and said, "I guess I'm all done for the day. I'm goin up. You comin, Patty?"

"I guess so." She stood and stretched. "Goodnight, Nellie."

"Goodnight. I'll close up down here."

Nellie didn't stay much longer. She thought Andy or Phyllis might come out, but she didn't see either of them. It was full dark now. She couldn't see well enough to go on with the mending, even with the porch light. It was time to be done for the day.

CHAPTER 5

From the top of the load, Andy watched as Crystal's little black VW Bug drove up the hill. It slowed and stopped. Crystal got out.

Andy slid down the bales of stacked hay and jumped to the ground. Crystal was already walking across the field toward him. Her skirt was light. It flowed around her legs as she walked. He didn't dare take a good look. He knew Pop and Gram and Phyllis were all watching and wondering.

He was so sweaty and dirty that he planned to stand downwind of her when she got close, but when she started talking, he forgot his plan.

"I told you I'd see you again. I want to help."

"But you can't…"

"Is that your sister driving the pickup?" Without waiting for an answer, she went over to the truck. Andy followed her. "Hi. My name's Crystal. What's yours? I came to help."

"Phyllis…"

"That's a beautiful name! What can I do, Phyllis?"

"Andy? She says she wants to help. What can she do? You've got to tell her."

"I don't know," he said weakly. "We're loaded. We need to take this hay to the barn."

"Okay," Phyllis said. "I'll drive. Get in, Crystal. You can ride."

Crystal looked at Andy to see what he thought, but he pretended not to notice, so she went around the truck and climbed in beside Phyllis.

Now Andy was torn two ways. Here was a chance to sit very close to Crystal, even closer than he had been when she gave him a ride the other day. But he was sweaty and covered with hay chaff. He should play it safe and walk up the hill. He got in the cab beside her. She had a spicy smell that he remembered from being in her car.

Phyllis had country music blaring on the radio. He wanted to turn it off, but he didn't know how Phyllis would react. He was afraid Crystal would think they were a family of hicks.

"Should we try to get some more bales on this load, Andy?"

"I don't think so. Let's unload these and come back."

"Who's that driving the tractor over there? Is that your mother?"

That made both Phyllis and Andy laugh. Phyllis said, "That's Gram. She rakes. Pop's runnin the baler."

When Phyllis put the truck in gear, it jumped and jerked and almost stalled. Andy had to brace his feet and hold onto the door to keep from crashing into Crystal. It smoothed out as they drove across the field, but the engine was roaring.

"You need to go into second gear, Phyllis."

"I know, but that's the one I have trouble with."

"You're goin to knock the bales off the back."

"Okay, here goes."

The truck jerked and then stalled.

Andy sighed. "Do you want me to drive?" He felt bad saying it. He knew Phyllis was trying to impress Crystal, and he didn't want to make her look stupid. Still, they had to get the load to the barn.

"I'm doin it, Andy. Just leave me alone." She started the truck and drove out of the field and onto the road in first gear. Going up the hill, she tried to go into second, but it stalled, so she drove up to the barn without shifting.

Andy managed not to say anything.

She stopped the truck in front of the barn. "Are we supposed to unload in the front, or around the back?"

"I don't know. I forgot to ask Pop."

"You better drive anyhow. I might could do it wrong."

They both got out. "You open the gates, Phyl. I'm goin round the back. We can unload in the middle. Pop'll be okay with that."

He got in the driver's seat. Crystal was still sitting close to the driver's side. She smiled at him and didn't move away when he got in. He drove around the back and up the ramp into the hayloft and shut off the engine. They both got out.

Phyllis walked up the ramp. "I'll throw the bales off, Andy."

"Okay. Give me your foot." He made a stirrup with his hands and gave her a boost. She scrambled the rest of the way and stood on top, ready to throw down bales.

She landed the first one hard and flat. Crystal hurried over and grabbed it by one string. Before Andy could stop her, she gave the string a jerk, and the bale burst open, scattering hay around the floor. She stopped still with a look of dismay on her face.

Andy hurried over to her. "That's all right," he said. He raised his hand to pat her comfortingly on the shoulder, before he realized that he didn't know her that well. He let his hand drop. "We always break some bales."

"But…" She looked so disappointed.

"You have to hold both strings at once."

Phyllis was watching from the top of the load.

"Put some bales down, Phyllis, so I can show her."

After that, things went better. It was very hot. The air was full of dust. They were all three coughing by the time the truck was empty. Crystal was covered with dirt and hay chaff, but she didn't seem to notice. She was having a good time.

Andy said, "I'm goin to back out. Phyl, you and Crystal stand in the doorway and stop me if I get too close to the edge."

As he backed away, they stood side by side, watching. They were talking. He hoped Phyllis wasn't saying bad things about him. He could ask her later, and he might get a straight answer.

When he was across the ramp and turned around, ready to go back to the field, he honked the horn, and they came running. Crystal climbed in beside him, and Phyllis went to get the gate.

"I like your sister," Crystal said.

"Be careful what you tell her—she's a blabbermouth."

"I don't care. I don't know anybody around here anyway. She can say whatever she wants."

They had three more loads after that, but they had a routine, and it went smoothly. By the time the last load was off, Andy was late for milking. He could hear Rosie bellowing for him. He had to hurry away.

He was milking when he heard Crystal behind him in the doorway.

"I wish I could stay for a milking lesson, but I'm so late as it is. My sister is going to kill me. I don't dare be any later. I'll be back soon for a lesson. I had so much fun today, and I learned so much. Thank you for letting me help." She said it all in a rush.

When he didn't hear any more, he looked around, but the doorway was empty.

Later, at supper, Pop said, "It's pretty decent hay. It registered two hundred fifty-six on the counter, and the baler didn't break more 'n three or four."

"We stacked 'em in the middle of the hayloft, Pop."

"That's good. What was that hippie woman doin here?"

"She was helpin us, Pop," Phyllis said. "She worked hard."

"Where'd she come from? What was she over here for?"

"She's a milk customer, or her sister is. The sister and her husband bought the Robinson farm."

"You mean the hippies that turned that place into a commune?"

"She says it ain't a commune."

"You just gotta take one look at her to know that ain't true."

Andy went on eating without looking up.

Gram said, "What difference does it make? She was very nice, and she helped a lot."

"She'd never had eggnog in the summer. She thought you were supposed to drink it at Christmastime. We surprised her. That was fun, wasn't it, Gram?"

"Yes, it was."

"But she liked it, didn't she? I liked her."

Andy felt Ma looking at him a couple of times, but he ducked his head and kept on eating. He didn't want to be part of the conversation.

CHAPTER 6

When Cynthia got out of the car with the bottle of milk, Laura was already on the porch, waiting for her.

"Where have you been all this time? I thought you were just going to run over to the Keyes farm to buy a bottle of milk. Did you have car trouble or something? I almost went out to look for you."

Cynthia was on the porch before Laura got quiet enough for her to reply. "I'm sorry. When I got over there, they were all out in the front field picking up bales of hay. I stopped to help them. It was lots of fun."

"You could have called me. I was really worried."

"I knew you'd be wondering where I was, but I don't know if they even have a telephone. I didn't go into their house."

"Well, listen, Cynthy. If you're going to be a lot later than you say, you need to find a way to let me know."

"Laura, I'm a grown-up. You know that. Why don't we say that you don't expect me until you see me? I can let you know if I'm in trouble or need your help."

"What do you think Mom would say? She probably thinks you're safe because you're with me."

"Oh God! It always comes back to that, doesn't it? Can't we leave Mom out of it? She's one of the main reasons why I didn't want to live at home this summer."

They walked into the kitchen. Laura went to the stove and started stirring something cooking there.

"That smells good. I'm starving."

"Call Bob and Paul. We've all been waiting for you."

"Bob's here?"

"He just got back. He's only staying a few days, and then he's heading for San Francisco. He's outside with Paul and Orion."

"I'll call them in a few minutes. I'm so dirty. I really need to take a shower before dinner."

"*Cynthia*, we've all been waiting forever. Don't make us wait any longer. Just do a quick clean up and call them. You can take a shower later."

When they were all sitting at the dinner table, Cynthia started to tell them about picking up the hay. She said how fun it was, but she also added that it was really hard work, and they all got sweaty and tired. "The grandmother came out with something for us to drink. You won't believe what it was." She looked around. She had everyone's attention. "What she brought us was a pitcher of eggnog!"

She was pleased to see their surprise. "Of course, it didn't have alcohol in it. I wasn't planning on having any. It seemed such a strange thing to drink when it was so hot, but they said it would take away my tiredness, and there was still more hay to be brought to the barn, so I had a glass, and it was true. I didn't feel tired after that. I was ready to go to work again. Isn't that strange?"

Later, when they were washing up, Laura said, "It's hard to believe eggnog could be so refreshing in the summer. It seems so heavy and wintery."

"I know, but it's so. You'll have to try it, and then you'll see for yourself. Their grandmother told me what was in it. I'll write it down when we get all done with the dishes. I like those blue eggs. They're nicer than the white ones from the store. That family knows about living on the land. I want to hang out with them a lot. We can learn so much from them." She didn't say anything about her attraction to Andy, but of course, that was a private part of the plan.

A couple of days later, when Cynthia went into the kitchen, Orion was in his highchair, concentrating on picking up bites of food from the slippery surface of his tray. Laura was washing dishes at the sink.

Cynthia said, "I have to go to the drugstore. Would you like me to pick up anything for you?"

Laura turned off the water and looked at her. "It's close to dinner time."

"Don't wait for me. I'm not sure how long I'll be gone."

"There's going to be rice pudding."

"I know. It smells really good."

"Why don't you stay so you can have some?"

"Save me a little. I'll have it when I get home."

"But, Cynthy, it's much better when it's warm."

"That's all right. I'll try to get back soon. I just don't want you to expect me."

She got in her car, thinking about how Andy could be milking when she got to the Keyes farm. As she drove up the road, she decided that if Andy wasn't there, she would buy some milk and leave.

She parked the car and walked around the corner of the barn. The door was open. She looked in. She was in luck. Andy was there, just like the first time she saw him. His back was to the door. He was milking the cow, swaying slightly back and forth. She could hear the squirts of milk hitting the pail.

She stood and watched. Should she say his name? Should she tap him on the shoulder? Should she just step up close and ask him if she could try it? She was still deciding what to do when he must have sensed her presence because he looked over his shoulder and saw her.

Right away he turned back to the cow, but Cynthia knew he wasn't milking any more. She couldn't hear the sound of the milk hitting the side of the pail. He knew she was there. It seemed stupid to say hello. She stepped up close beside him and said, "Are you going to teach me how to do that, or not?"

He said something she didn't catch as he jumped up. He might have been telling her to sit down. She wasn't sure, but she sat down on the stool anyway. The cow was so close that she could feel the heat from her body.

In a minute Andy was back with an empty bucket. He turned it upside down and sat on it. She looked at him with a question. His eyes were gray and deep. He was so close. It was almost a prelude to a kiss.

But after a minute of looking at each other, Cynthia reached out and grabbed hold of one of the cow's teats. It was warm and a little bit sticky. She squeezed it, but nothing happened. She tried again, but still nothing. Then she reached out for the other one with her other hand and squeezed that several times. Still nothing. "Maybe there's no more milk in there."

Andy took the teats and milked a few streams from each of them. He looked at her.

"Well, what am I doing wrong, then?" she said.

"Here. Give me your hand."

Their shoulders had been touching, but they had not yet touched each other on purpose. Cynthia held out her hand.

He grabbed her index finger with his fist and squeezed it. "Do you feel that?"

She nodded. Of course, she did.

"Well, that's the milkin motion."

She didn't like to say that she had been so distracted by him holding her hand that she didn't know what motion she felt.

"You kinda bump before you squeeze. Try it that way."

"Do it again so I can feel the bump."

He did. "Can you feel it?"

"Maybe. I'm not sure." He was still holding her finger. "Let me try it." She put both hands on the cow's teats and tried to bump and squeeze, but still no milk would come out.

The cow was stepping around and shaking her head, rattling the metal bar around her neck.

Andy said, "She's gettin restless. I better finish her off. She's goin to start kickin in a minute."

Cynthia sat back, but she stayed close to the cow and Andy, so she could see what he was doing. She couldn't see much. It looked so easy when he did it.

Andy stood. He picked up the pail of milk and set it out of the way. He was just going to open the metal bar around the cow's neck when Phyllis appeared in the doorway.

"Hey Andy, I been lookin…what're you doin? Is that Crystal? Hey Crystal, are you doin Andy's milkin for him?"

"I would if I knew how."

"Then what're you sittin under there for?"

Cynthia stood up. "Andy was trying to show me, but I couldn't make the milk come out."

"Oh, it's easy," Phyllis said. "I can teach you."

Andy said, "I got to put her out with the others." He looked at Phyllis. "You don't have to stay."

"Andy, you got a postcard from the guys. Don't you want to see it?"

"I'll get it later."

"They all signed it. They're goin to be in basic for eight weeks. They think you can catch up before they have to go to Vietnam."

"I'll see it when I come up to the house."

"Andy, they all signed it!"

"You're not supposed to read other people's mail."

"It's a postcard. Anybody can read a postcard. There's a picture of a tank on it."

"Okay, Phyllis, you can go now. I'll get the postcard later."

"I could stay and keep you company while Crystal's here."

Cynthia said, "Thanks Phyllis, but I have to get home right away. I just want to ask Andy something, and then I'm leaving. You go on."

"Well...okay, but come back soon, and I'll teach you how to milk. Andy can't teach you as good as I can."

"Thanks. I'll see you soon, Phyllis."

"Okay. Don't forget."

Cynthia was standing in the same spot when Andy came back. He looked expectant. He obviously had no idea what she wanted to ask him about.

She didn't hesitate. "The guys that wrote that postcard—are they friends of yours?"

"Yeah. I guess so. Guys in my class anyhow."

"And they're going to Vietnam?"

"That's what they say." While they talked, he was straightening up the room without looking at her.

"And you're going too?"

"That's the plan."

"Don't you know it's wrong to go to Vietnam?"

"You have to go where they tell you to go."

37

They looked at each other for a minute. Then Cynthia said, "I guess I didn't know that about you. This changes things."

"And anyhow, it ain't like I got a choice."

She had to remember that she hardly knew him, and yet, when she saw the disappointment on his face, she wanted to touch him. "When they signed up, did they *know* they would have to go to Vietnam?"

"They knew they'd get drafted if they didn't sign up. We all know who can get out of the draft and who has to go whether they want to or not."

"And you?"

"I ain't got no choice either. I'm goin to sign up in September."

She thought he was being evasive because he didn't want her to know he was younger than she was. But she already knew that, and she didn't care. It was his willingness to go to war that she couldn't deal with. Laura would say this is what happens when you get mixed up with people who are different from you. It served her right for crossing those lines. It was time to get out of there.

She didn't say any more. She just turned and left, without even looking back. When she got to her car, she jumped in and peeled off, going fast down the hill.

She was on the edge of bursting into tears all the way home, trying to hold it back until she could get to the privacy of her room. It made her realize how much she had wanted to spend time with Andy and his family, learning how to live on the land the way they did.

When she went into the kitchen, Bob was there, talking to Laura. Cynthia was going to nod hello and keep on going, but Laura stopped her.

"Hi, Cynthy, Bob just got his car back from the mechanic, and it's bad news. The transmission is leaking so badly that he can't keep fluid in it, and it would be a big job, more than the car is worth, to fix it."

Bob said, "It's history, that's for sure. He thinks there's a crack in the block too."

Cynthia stopped with her hand on the door to the back stairs. She sighed. "I'm sorry, Bob, I know you were looking forward to your cross-country trip."

"Oh, I'm still going to go. It's too good to miss. I can always hitchhike if I have to."

Cynthia stood there with her hand on the door, thinking of her own situation and how she could face it the way Bob was. It was different, of course. She had to find a new direction because she couldn't pursue the old one. Then she heard herself say, "Suppose we went together?"

"Wow!" Bob said. "It's like the old saying, 'When one door shuts, another one opens.' Would you really consider it?"

"Sure. I haven't completely settled on what I'm going to do this summer." She looked past Bob and saw the dismay on Laura's face. "Does that worry you, Laura?"

"Yes, but I…it's not for me to tell you what to do."

"You're not. I asked you."

"Well, I was just wondering how to explain it to Mom."

"Oh look, Laura, we can't let Mom control us. That settles it. I'm ready to go, Bob, whenever you are." She didn't want to give Laura a chance to object. "What you said about one door closing and another opening is the perfect metaphor for our trip."

"It's going to take me a couple of days to deal with my old car."

"That's okay. I want to get mine checked out too. A couple of days sounds perfect."

So that was how they left it. Cynthia saw the worry on Laura's face. "It's okay, Laura. Mom won't blame you for not stopping me. I'll tell her that you didn't want me to go, and I went anyway. She'll understand. I've done that to *her* often enough."

After that she was able to escape to her room to have a good cry. But she didn't feel like crying any more. The new door was opening wide, and she was going to walk through it without looking back.

CHAPTER 7

When Andy got back to the milking room after putting Rosie out to pasture, Crystal was standing in the doorway, outlined in the soft evening light. It was like the first time he saw her. He thought he should pull her into the shadowy room and put his arms around her. He almost did it too. Phyllis was gone, and they were alone. But before he could make a move, she started talking.

She was angry. She wanted some answers. Did his friends know they were going to be sent to Vietnam? And what was *he* going to do?

He told her the truth. He didn't have time not to. He said they knew what they were doing. They wanted to go to Vietnam to defend their country and fight Communism. He was planning to join them in September. He hoped she would see from what he said that they could have the summer to be together, but she wasn't thinking about the possibilities for the two of them, and even if she had been, when he stupidly said they all knew who could get out of the draft and who couldn't, his chances with her were over.

She didn't say anything. She just turned around and left. By the time he got to the door, she was going around the corner of the barn. He grabbed the pail of milk and followed her, but when he got to the parking area, she was in her car and backing up. She gunned it down the drive without even looking in his direction. And that was the end of that.

If Phyllis hadn't butted in when she did, or if the postcard hadn't arrived when it did, the subject of Vietnam wouldn't have come up. Still, he had to admit that sooner or later she would have found out that he was planning to sign up as soon as he could, and that he wanted to go fight for his country the way Pop had fought in World War II. He needed to look at it like that, since he didn't really have a choice.

If he'd been able to think clearly when she was nearby, he would have known that she was against the war. All the hippies were. Everybody said so. But he hadn't been thinking about anything except that she was so beautiful and so close. For just a little while, it looked like this summer was going to be a time he could remember when he was on the other side of the world fighting for freedom in the jungle.

He felt miserable all the next day, dodging Phyllis's endless questions about Crystal and when she was going to come over to learn how to milk.

In the evening he managed to give Phyllis the slip and go up to his trail through the woods. He carried a small ax with him, even though he knew there was no longer any reason to work on the trail. It was close to dark, but there was enough light to see the path.

He went over the hill to the Robinsons' back field. The house below was all lit up, but there weren't any people around. He sat under an old apple tree and watched for a while. There was a hole in his heart, and he realized how much of the last weeks he had spent thinking of his impossible fantasy about Crystal.

The next two days he had to help Pop get parts for the baler and put them in. The whole time he thought about getting away to the woods. Pop was in an awful mood about the baler breakdown. Andy couldn't seem to do anything right.

By suppertime of the second day, they had the baler ready again, and the night was supposed to be clear. Pop was in a much better mood. After supper when he went to watch the television news, and Ma, Phyllis, and Gram were all in the kitchen cleaning up, Andy had a chance to get away unnoticed.

When he stepped from the field onto the trail under the trees, he knew why he had been wishing to get there. It was a different world in the woods, no need to hurry, no being wrong, no being scolded and called stupid, just quiet and peace. Even losing Crystal before he had found her was different and almost all right.

He walked over to the Robinsons' field and sat down under the apple tree. It took him a while to realize that someone was working in the garden. It took him another while to see that it was Crystal, and she was alone. It was too good a chance to miss.

He started walking down the field slowly, wondering what she was going to do when she looked up and saw him. His heart was beating fast. Once she stretched and moved to a new spot. He was sure she would notice that he was there, but she was looking toward the house and didn't turn in his direction. He had never seen her so messy and dirty, but it just made her more beautiful. He got all the way down to the garden and then stood there watching her weeding for a few minutes before she looked around and saw him.

She dropped the hoe. "You," she said. "I don't believe it. I was just thinking about you. How did you get here?" But before he could answer, she started talking again. "I went over to your place yesterday to say goodbye, but no one was home."

"Goodbye?" he said stupidly.

"Yes. I wanted to fix the bad feelings between us before I left. I guess that was silly of me."

"You're leaving?" he said. She was going to think he was a moron.

"I'm leaving tomorrow morning to go to the Summer of Love in San Francisco. I've always wanted to drive across the country. I'm not sure what we're going to do for money, but I guess we'll figure it out along the way."

"We...?"

"I'm going with a friend of my sister's."

For a minute, he thought it was a girlfriend, and he was going to say something about how dangerous that would be.

But then she went on. "He's been planning this trip for a while, but his car had too much wrong with it, so he sold it for fifty dollars. He was going to hitchhike, but I said I'd like to go. I don't know if my little car will make it all the way, but we'll find out."

"Is he your boyfriend?" He couldn't believe he asked such a question. It just came out.

"Bob?" She laughed. "No, of course not. He's just a friend, a person to travel with. But how'd you get here, anyway? You must have walked past all of them."

"I came down the back field from the woods. I told you there was a trail from your woodlot to ours."

"Really? I guess I forgot."

"We get firewood up there, and the Robinsons used to. Sometimes we'd see them when we were both workin at the same time."

"There's a road from your house to ours?"

"A woods road. It ain't like a town road."

"I would love to see it."

"I'd show you if you were goin to be here."

"What about right now?"

"Now?"

"Do you have time?"

"Well, yeah…but it's goin to be dark soon."

"I'm not scared of the dark." She was smiling at him now. "Are you?"

"Me? I'm never scared in the woods."

"Well, let's go then. I want to see your trail, and this is my only chance."

"You need shoes," he said. "The ground is rough."

"I've got some. Don't worry." She sat in the dirt on the edge of the garden and started to put on her sandals.

They weren't the right shoes for a walk in the woods, but he didn't say anything. It could jeopardize his last chance to be alone with her.

She smiled at him and reached out her hand for him to help her to her feet, and when he pulled her up, they were standing very close together. She apparently had forgotten all he had said about Vietnam.

"Let's go," she said, and they walked up the field so close together that sometimes their shoulders touched. He would have taken her hand, but he was conscious that someone might be watching them from the house.

There were several times when one of her sandals came off, and she had to stop and sit down in the tall grass to put it on again, while he stood there waiting, feeling as though there was a target on his back, and that everyone in the house below was wondering what he was doing there.

It seemed to take forever to get to the top of the field and the old apple on the tree line. He hurried them past it and into the woods.

Now he could take her hand, and he did. They walked a little way up the Robinsons' overgrown logging road in the dusky light.

Suddenly she stopped and stood still. "I had no idea," she said. She turned in a slow circle, looking up at the trees overhead. "Here I was living right beside this beautiful place, and I didn't even know it. It's like a church, but much better. You don't have to get dressed up and worry what people are going to think. Look how dirty I am, and it doesn't even matter." She took his hand again. "Show me more. I want to see everything."

He wanted to kiss her, but he could tell that it wasn't the right time. "This road goes straight up the hill to a stone wall at the top. That's the property line. Our loggin road goes down to our back field on the other side of the hill."

She took his hand in both of hers. "Show me."

He was trying hard to be the sensible one. "I think we can walk to the stone wall and back to your field before full dark."

She said, "There's so much to explore in the forest. I feel like Hansel and Gretel. Don't you?"

He smiled down at her. He felt a lot of different things, but that wasn't one of them. While he worked on the trail on his side of the hill, he had pictured them walking side by side, holding hands and talking. He never thought it would actually happen, but here they were. At the same time, he felt sad. This was the beginning, and it was also the end. "I wish you weren't leaving tomorrow," he said.

She squeezed his hand. "I know. Me too."

When they got to the stone wall, she climbed to the top of it and stood there. "I feel like I'm the king of the world. Let's keep going."

"We need to get back to your field before it gets darker. There ain't goin to be a moon until later." He reached out his hand, and she took it and climbed down. He kissed her then. She would have stayed there kissing, but he was worried about them getting off the trail in the dark.

"Come on," he said. "We've got to go."

They walked down the hill with their arms around each other, laughing when one or the other of them stumbled over a root or some obstruction on the trail.

At the apple tree, they stopped and looked at the house below with all its lights blazing. Andy suddenly realized that it was over, that she was going to walk down the field and out of his life, because even if she came back after her trip out west, he would be gone, on his way to Vietnam.

Desperation made him bold, and he began to kiss her with everything he had. She kissed back eagerly. He didn't think about anything. It was his last chance. Soon they were lying on the ground under the tree with their bodies touching everywhere.

But when Andy began to undo her blue jeans, she pushed him away. "No, I can't," she said. She began to cry. He watched as she struggled to her feet and started down the field. She didn't even say goodbye.

He sat there for a long time, breathing hard. Then he got to his feet and started for home. It was a slow trip through the dark woods, but he needed time to get himself calmed down.

CHAPTER 8

Cynthia pushed Andy away and got to her feet. Everything was all mixed up and out of control. She thought she was making her own decisions, but other people, including Andy, kept doing things she hadn't anticipated.

She would have loved to stay there, but it was happening too fast and at the wrong time. She thought she was saying goodbye, and now she didn't know what to do. Leaving seemed to be the only option, and she didn't want to leave. She hurried down the field, stumbling over her sandals and crying. She had made a mess of everything.

When she got almost to the house, she realized that crying wasn't going to help. She was dirty from the garden work and disheveled from the lovemaking. She needed to get to her room without being seen.

She had no idea what time it was, but there were lots of lights on, so they were still awake, and Laura was probably wondering where she was. Laura would want to spend some time with her before she left with Bob. And she hadn't even started to pack up her things. She would have to take everything because she didn't know when she was coming back. Why did she tell Bob she would go with him? She really didn't want to.

She slipped in by the front door, which no one ever used, and managed to get to her little room without being seen. They were talking in the kitchen below. She could hear their voices. She cleaned herself up and changed clothes and went downstairs to join them. They were surprised to see her.

Orion was in his highchair. Laura was feeding him a bedtime snack. "Oh, here you are, Cynthy. I was wondering. Where have you been?"

"Upstairs getting my things together, and before that, I was out in the garden, weeding the corn. I wanted to finish it before I left, but there's still half a row to do."

"You were weeding in the dark?"

"I had to stop when I couldn't see what I was doing. I'm sorry I didn't get it all done."

"That's okay. It was nice of you to do as much as you did."

Bob and Paul were talking about things that Bob wanted to store for the summer. They went out together to find a good place in the barn.

Laura wiped Orion's face and picked him up. She looked over at Cynthia and smiled. Then she said, "Have you been crying, Cynthy?"

"Just a little. I'm sad to be going away. I love it here."

"You don't *have* to go."

"I know, but I said I would, and Bob's counting on my car."

"That's not a good reason."

"I know. I'm so confused. Every time I think I know what direction to take, things change, and I get mixed up again." She knew as she was saying the words that they didn't make much sense.

Laura gave her a funny look, and she wondered how she could explain herself without mentioning Andy, but just then, Orion saved the situation by starting to cry.

Laura said, "I hate to stop this conversation. I want to know what's bothering you, but right now I have to nurse Orion and get him into bed. Maybe we could talk later?"

Cynthia nodded, even though she didn't know how she could explain what she was feeling without saying more than she wanted to say.

She went up the back stairs to the little storeroom where she had been staying since Mom and Dad's visit. Laura kept trying to get her to move to a nicer room, but she was happy where she was. There was a folding cot to sleep on. She felt as though she was camping out amid the boxes piled around. But what she liked best was the back stairway that led from the storeroom down to the kitchen. She could come and go as she pleased without anyone knowing.

After a while, Laura called to her from the bottom of the stairs. "Are you up there, Cynthy?"

"Yes. I'm packing."

Laura's head appeared and then the rest of her as she climbed the stairs. She sat on the top step and looked at Cynthia. "I just wanted you to know that both Paul and I would love to have you stay all summer if you wanted to. Please don't leave because you think we want you to go."

"I know, Laura, and I appreciate it. That isn't the reason I'm going."

"What is it then?"

"I'm not sure anymore. Isn't that stupid? I guess I thought I could help Bob out, and it sounded like a great road trip."

"You have to decide what you want, but just so you know, we'll be glad if you decide to stay. Paul and I already talked about it."

"Thanks. I *do* know."

Laura got to her feet. "I'm going to bed. Maybe we can talk some more in the morning, but tell me one thing before I leave—what made you change your mind?"

There was that question she couldn't answer again. "Let's talk in the morning, Laura. I hope it'll be clearer then."

"Okay, Cynthy. Sleep well."

After Laura left, Cynthia stuffed everything into her backpack, and when the house got quiet, she took a shower. Up until then, she could smell Andy on her skin, but after the shower he was gone, and that made her cry again.

She went back to her room and got into bed, but she still didn't know what she was going to do. She lay there fretting, going back and forth in her mind and getting nowhere. She could tell Laura that Andy said he was planning to join the army, and that he wanted to go to Vietnam to fight. She could say that she knew Laura was right when she said that people like the Keyes family, like a lot of old-time Vermonters, were very conservative and in favor of the war, and that made an unbridgeable divide between them and us. Laura would understand that.

But the next part—the magical walk in the forest at night and the lovemaking—that would be harder to explain. She really wanted to spend the summer with Andy, getting to know his world, and she really believed she could make him understand what a mistake the war in Vietnam was. She could save his life. She couldn't get Laura to understand that part, and anyway, she didn't want Laura to know about Andy. Even she didn't know much about him, except that he was different from any boyfriend she had ever had. She lay there, thinking about walking in the woods with him, about kissing him. She thought about how strong he was in spite of being so thin. That gave her a shiver of pleasure.

Then she thought about how Bob was going to wake her early in the morning so they could leave. If she decided not to go, she would have to tell him then, probably in front of Laura and Paul.

Later—she must have been asleep, because when she woke up, it was very still, with a stillness that had a late-night quality to it. She went to the bathroom and then stood in the hallway. Somewhere someone was snoring.

She went down the hall on tiptoe and opened the door to Bob's room. She didn't dare make much noise, so she had to say his name a few times before he woke up enough to hear her.

Finally, he said, "Huh? What? Who?" She could hear the covers rustling as he turned over.

"It's me, Cynthia."

"Oh," he said. "I see. That's nice." And he raised the covers, so she could get under.

"No, Bob. It's not like that. I need to talk to you."

He put the covers down and pushed himself up higher in the bed. "What's the matter?"

A little light came into the room from the hall. Cynthia could see the shape of him. There wasn't enough light to see his face, only the white disk of it against the headboard of the bed. She didn't want to shut the door because she wouldn't have been able to see anything.

Suddenly she felt very tired. She said, "Can I sit down?"

"Sure." He moved his legs over. "You can get under the covers too if you want to."

"No thanks. I have to tell you something."

"Okay. What's the problem?"

"I can't go with you."

"Oh," he said, and then he was quiet for a minute. "Why not? I thought we were all set."

"I thought so too, until I started to pack my stuff. That was when I realized that I didn't want to leave."

"It's going to be a good road trip. Are you sure?"

"I've been sitting in my room, crying. That's how sure I am."

"Okay, Cynthia. I don't want to force you…if you're sure."

"Thanks for being so nice about it. I hope you have a great trip." She stood up and went to the door.

"Cynthia, wait a minute."

"What?"

"Look in my pack. It's right there by the desk. My weed and pipe and papers and everything is in that compartment in the back."

"That's okay, Bob."

"No, you take it. If I'm going to hitchhike, I can't have it on me. If you don't want it, you can give it to Laura and Paul."

She pulled the pack over to the light and found all his smoking paraphernalia. "Are you sure, Bob?"

"Of course. Enjoy. I can't carry it if I'm hitching."

"Have a great trip. I'll probably be sorry I missed it. And thanks for the weed." She went back to her own room. At least it was settled, and she was going to do what she felt like doing, even if it was a mistake. She hid Bob's weed in her pack. She liked having it, even though she wasn't sure she wanted to use it.

When she woke up, the sun was pouring through her window, making a bright square on the floor. She lay there, looking at the shaft of light and the specks of dust dancing in it. She moved her hand, and the specks all changed direction. It had to be late in the morning, but she couldn't hear any noises from downstairs. She dressed and went down to the kitchen. There were dishes in the sink and coffee in the unplugged coffee pot. She poured herself a cup and sat on the porch steps in the sun to drink it, toasting herself in the sunlight. The only car parked out in front was hers.

She didn't have to do anything or go anywhere. She could just sit in the sunshine and grow like a plant. Birds were singing in the trees. Flies were buzzing across the porch. A wasp landed near her and walked along the step with its feelers out, exploring.

She was still sitting in the same place when Laura drove up. She watched Laura get Orion out of his booster seat and carry him to the porch.

"Hi, Cynthy. I'm glad you're up. Take Orion, will you? I have groceries to unload." She handed Orion to Cynthia and went back to the car.

Orion was sticky from the treats he'd been eating. He squirmed until she set him down on the porch floor. She didn't dare leave him to help Laura with the groceries.

Laura walked by with her arms full. "Did you get yourself some coffee?"

"There was a little left in the pot."

"Ugh! It must have been cold."

"That's okay. I didn't care."

"Just let me grab the last few bags, and I'll make us a fresh pot."

When Laura had the coffee ready, she put Orion in his highchair with some Cheerios and chopped strawberries on his tray. She sat beside Cynthia on the steps.

"Did Bob tell you that I wasn't going with him?"

"Yes, he said you changed your mind, and he was going to hitchhike. I took him out to the highway on my way to the grocery store."

"I realized last night that I wanted to be here. I went to Bob's room and told him. I didn't want to leave it up in the air. After that I could finally get some sleep."

"He said he'd be back tonight if he didn't get a ride."

"I hope he'll have good luck. I feel guilty not going with him. Did he have a lot of stuff to carry?"

"He left some more in the barn this morning. He only had his pack and his guitar."

"I'm glad he took his guitar."

"I didn't tell Mom about your trip. I knew she would want me to talk you out of it, so I decided I would wait until you were on the road before I said anything. Now I don't have to. She would have asked me a lot of questions I couldn't answer, like what was your exact route and where were you going to stay."

"I liked Bob's idea of leaving it up to chance or fate or whatever happened to come along."

"I can understand that, but can you imagine trying to explain it to Mom?"

Cynthia laughed.

"I was afraid she would ask me if you were going to marry him."

"When I got to UMass last fall, I told everyone my name was Crystal. I still haven't had the nerve to tell Mom. Cynthia is so old-fashioned."

"I don't like my name either. I keep trying to get Paul to call me Laurel, but he always forgets."

"I'll try to remember to call you that. After a while, it starts to feel natural."

"Guess who I saw in the grocery store this morning."

"I'm no good at guessing. Who?"

"Angela."

"I don't know *anybody* named Angela."

"Remember the night before Mom and Dad came to visit? Those two women who had to spend the night here, because one of them was trying to get away from her boyfriend? Angela something. I don't remember her last name. Did she even tell us? Well, anyway, that's who it was. She looked quite happy. I thought she was going to say she had finally gotten away from the awful boyfriend, but no, she's back with him again, and she didn't even make him get rid of the guns. Can you believe it?"

"Oh sure, I believe it. That's always the way it is."

"I wonder if Orion is going to hate *his* name. When we were driving to the hospital, we could see the belt of Orion in the dawn sky. It was so beautiful that we decided right then, if the baby was a boy, we would name him Orion."

"I love it. Maybe he will too."

"It's too late now, anyway."

"In some ways, Mom and Dad force us to rebel by wanting us to stay the same. You can't. You have to change. You have to have room to grow."

"I can understand Mom and Dad a little better now that I have Orion. It's scary being a parent. You want so much for your child, and you can see danger everywhere."

"I know, Laura...I mean, Laurel, but you aren't holding Orion back. You want him to try new things. You want him to learn and grow."

"I hope so...but it's different. Anyway, tell me about your plans. What are you going to do now that you're staying here?"

"I don't know. Maybe nothing, maybe I'll just be here...until you get sick of me."

"That's not going to happen, not ever."

Cynthia put her arm around her. "I can't believe how lucky I am to have you for a sister."

After a few minutes, Orion began to get restless. Laura stood up. "Okay, Orion, I know you need changing, and there are all the groceries still to put away."

Cynthia said, "I can do the groceries. I'll put away everything I can."

"Thanks. That would help."

In the afternoon, Cynthia went to the garden to finish the row of corn. It was so quiet. She worked along, chopping weeds with the hoe, until she happened to look up the field at the tree line and the woods beyond it. She thought about last night and Andy. He could be there behind the trees, watching, but she knew he wasn't. He thought she left this morning for California. She needed to let him know that she had changed her mind.

She could hear the long-drawn call of the mourning dove. There were two of them calling to each other, a call and response. One was in the trees at the top of the field in the direction of the Keyes farm. She thought of that one as Andy, calling to her, since the other bird was near the house. It was a song of loneliness and longing.

She walked up the field to the woods. It took a few minutes of searching, but then she found a place where the plants were bent over by someone stepping on them, and she knew she had found the path.

She was pleased with her woodcraft. Maybe she didn't need Andy to teach her about the woods. She could find her own way.

Under the trees, it was much cooler than it was in the bright field. Here was the place where the woods opened up so that it felt like a cathedral. She wasn't afraid of getting lost. She felt confident that she would recognize the trail. She went slowly up the hill, looking around. She could smell earth and leaves and the sharp scent of pine. There were bright patches on the ground where the sun came through the leaves. The bright spots danced in the breeze. Everything was alive and in motion, and at the same time, everything was still.

After a while, she began to feel that she was being watched. At first, she thought Andy might be nearby, but then she realized that he would show himself and say something. It had to be a wild creature, maybe many wild creatures, animals that knew she was there in their territory, animals that were waiting for her to go away. She didn't know what lived in the forest. There might even be bears.

She wasn't very far up the hill, but it was enough. She turned around and hurried back down the way she had come. When she burst through the last trees and bushes out into the bright field, it felt warm and safe. She was back in a world she knew. She walked slowly through the tall grass. It felt like walking through water. When she got to the garden, she was glad to work on the corn again.

The next day in the afternoon Cynthia went over to the Keyes farm. It was a very different kind of a day. Yesterday had been all summer sunshine, but today there was a light, steady rain. She picked her time carefully, and she was in luck. A few minutes after she pulled up, Andy came around the corner of the barn with the milk pail.

The look on his face was what she had come for. He nearly dropped the pail, and his face started to get red. He recovered a little and came over to her car.

His confusion made her smile. "Remember me?" she said.

"I thought you left a few days ago."

"I was going to, but I changed my mind. I haven't learned how to milk yet. Are you still going to teach me?"

"Yes. I want to." He raised the pail a little. "But I can't today. I've already milked. Do you want to do somethin tonight?"

"Okay."

"Is it all right if we take your car?"

"Sure."

"I could meet you at the bottom of the hill in a couple of hours. What about seven-thirty?"

"I can come up the hill and meet you here. Then you won't get wet."

"Down by the road is better. If they see your car, I'll have a lot of explainin to do. Phyllis is always tryin to spy on me. This way I can just say I'm goin downstreet."

"Okay, then. Seven-thirty, at the bottom of the hill." She was pleased. She drove away singing Maria's song, "Tonight," from *West Side Story*.

CHAPTER 9

When Nellie was cleaning up the kitchen after lunch, Frank came in to say he had to go to the auto parts store. She had planned to work in the garden, but it was a gray day with a soft rain falling. It was a good day to visit Helen. She hadn't been to see her for quite a while. Frank was ready to leave. She just had time to put on a clean dress and grab a dozen of her freshest eggs.

Helen's creaky little house was the same as ever. Frank waited while Nellie knocked on the door. She looked through the glass and saw Helen coming to answer, so she waved to Frank that he could leave.

Helen unlocked the door and opened it. "Why Nellie," she said. "I didn't expect you. You should've called to tell me you were comin."

Nellie gave her a quick kiss on her soft and wrinkly cheek. "I took a chance. I didn't have time to call. Frank was in a hurry as usual."

"Come in. Where is Frank?"

"He's gone to do some errands downstreet. You'll see him when he comes to pick me up."

She followed Helen to the cluttered front room. All the windows were closed, and the air was musty. Helen turned off the television as she went by. "If I had known you were comin to visit, I could of baked somethin for you."

"You don't need to treat me like a guest. I'm not interruptin one of your television programs, am I?"

"Oh no. I'm so glad to see you. I just had it on for company. I like to hear the voices when I'm alone."

She hated to see the way Helen lived, all cooped up, especially when there was a soft, summery rain outside, but she couldn't say so. "Your yard looks real nice."

"My boys keep it up for me. I can't do it myself anymore." There was a moment of silence, and then Helen jumped up. "I don't know what's the matter with my manners. Even if you are my big sister, I could get you a glass of iced tea."

"It's okay, Helen. I'm fine. I came to see how you are and to hear your news. I don't need refreshments."

"I'll be right back. Just stay there."

So Nellie stayed where she was, looking around the room. It hadn't changed in years. Some of the furniture and some of the pictures on the wall came from their childhood home. Helen seemed frail and old. Nellie thought she really ought to get in to see her more often. She felt younger and stronger than Helen even though she was two years older.

When Helen came back into the room, carrying two glasses of iced tea on a little tray, Nellie said, "Do you see much of Mabel? How's she doin?"

"We talk every couple of days. She's busy right now. She's plannin to fly to California to see Marjorie and her husband and their children. She's worried about the trip."

"I would be too. That's a long way."

"She can do it. She's younger than we are. How's your family?"

"Well, you know about Andy's graduation. Did you get the invitation?"

"I did. I'm sorry I didn't make it. Was it nice?"

"It was fine, except pretty soon he'll be eighteen. Then he'll be drafted, and that means Vietnam."

"Does he want to go?"

"It's hard to say. Frank thinks he does, but I don't know. Sometimes he asks me questions that make me wonder." She didn't want to tell Helen about his hippie girlfriend. She could just imagine what Helen would say about that. "Oh goodness, I brought you some eggs, and I forgot about them. They're still in the truck."

"Some of your famous blue ones?"

"That's right."

"Oh good. I love your eggs. They keep for such a long time."

"That's because they're fresh. I just added on some beautiful young hens this spring. I might even take a few to Tunbridge this fall. I could win some prizes."

"Oh Nellie, you try to do too much."

"When fall comes, I'll have to do more. Andy will be gone."

"But you should be thinkin of retirin, not addin on more work. Why don't you leave the farm to Frank and move back to town? You could live here. I have plenty of room. We'd get along fine, and you could take it easy. There's not much work."

Nellie secretly shuddered at the thought. To be shut away from light and air and weather, from rain and snow and the starry night sky—just thinking about it made her feel like crying. "Thank you, Helen. It's nice that you want me, but what would I do with my chickens? I couldn't bring them. Your neighbors wouldn't like it."

"You could leave them out at the farm. Frank could take care of them. You could go out and visit them whenever you wanted to."

"I couldn't do that. Frank has too much to do already. Suppose some of them got sick? I need to check on them every day. Think of how long it's been since I had time to come see you. Besides, I have work out there, and I wouldn't have nothin to do in here."

Helen said, "Oh for heaven's sakes. If you wanted somethin to do, you could go back to nursin. You were such a hero during the Spanish flu. I wanted to be just like you. You saved lives. Everyone said so. People always need nurses."

"That was a different world. I couldn't be a nurse now. Everythin has changed. I would have to go back to school and start over. I'm too old, and it would cost a lot of money. And anyway, I've never regretted giving up nursin to buy the farm with Phil. Frank and I were just saying the other day how glad we were that we didn't sell out and move into town when Phil died. Remember how you and Mabel and Ma tried to get us to do that?"

"Oh yes. We all worried about you. Remember that awful old hired hand you had?"

"Eddie Slocum? He *was* awful, old and unfit, and on top of that, he was a drunk, but I had no choice. I needed help, and everyone able-bodied was gone to the war."

"You shouldn't have tried to keep the farm goin without Frank. That's what we kept tryin to make you understand."

"There's no sense in talkin about it all these years later, but just let me say that I managed to do it. The war ended, and Frank came home, and a few years later, we even got electricity, and everythin is so much easier. We're in great shape now, and we'll do fine, even if Andy gets drafted."

"Charlie's boys *wanted* to go to Vietnam. I think they thought it was a chance for adventure. Johnny is going to be home pretty soon. Maybe Andy ought to just go in and get it over with, like they did."

"And fight in a war even if he thinks it's wrong?"

"Is that what he thinks? Is that what you think, Nellie?"

Nellie sighed. "No. I don't know. I don't know what to think. It seems so far away."

"Well, no one could argue about that."

"It don't seem to have anythin to do with us. I can't see the point."

"The last war was far away too," said Helen.

"You mean Korea?"

"No. World War II. We all knew what we were fighting for in that one."

"That was different."

"I know. It seems different to me too, but maybe it's because we're gettin old. We don't understand how necessary it is. Our government thinks this war is important. My boys think so. They say I don't know enough, and that I'd better be quiet or someone might think I was siding with the hippies. I don't want that. Charlie's going to get me a flag to hang on my front porch. I hope he'll do it before the Fourth and then we'll leave it up, and everyone will know what that means."

Just as Nellie was about to say something about how Frank had a big flag on their porch, Frank himself drove up. Nellie saw his pickup go by the window. She hurried out to the kitchen to open the door for him. He dutifully went in to say hello to Helen, but he wouldn't sit down. He said he had to get home to put the parts on the tractor before dark.

Nellie ran out to the truck to get Helen's eggs. She put them on the kitchen table, and she and Frank started maneuvering toward the door, with Helen either politely or genuinely trying to get them to stay longer.

Out in the truck, riding home, Nellie said, "She wants me to move into town with her."

"That's not the first time we've heard that."

"I know. What would I do all day? She sits in that stuffy little room with all the windows closed. I'd go crazy."

"You can tell her no, Ma. You've done that before."

"I know. Thanks, Frank."

After supper was cleaned up, Nellie turned off the kitchen light and went down the hall to the front room. Frank was in there watching the television news. She stopped for a minute, but it didn't look interesting. For a change it wasn't Vietnam. It was a riot in Buffalo with lots of sirens and police, worlds away from Vermont, where everyone had their own troubles, different from the ones on television. She got her sewing basket and her glasses and the shirt she was mending.

On the porch, she put the basket beside the rocker and sat down with the shirt across her lap. It felt good to be all done, even though she hadn't done that much today, what with going to town to see Helen and all.

It was still daylight, but the light was gray and muted because of the rain. She looked out across the fields and the valley to the hills and the line of mountains in the distance.

A while later Frank and Patty came out to join her. They all sat quietly, listening to the soft sound of the rain. No birds were singing. They had finished mating and were into the hard work of feeding their new families.

Nellie said, "I guess the birds are too busy these days to make much noise. They don't want to notify the whole world about where their nests are. If you think about it, they take some big risks in the spring when they mate. Every time they tell the females where they're at, they're also tellin the predators. Love is a risky business."

Frank said, "That's crazy, Ma. You act like they have a choice."

"Who knows? Maybe they do."

Patty said, "Andy sure was in a good mood at the supper table tonight."

"I noticed that. Somethin changed since yesterday."

Frank said, "I don't know what you mean. He acted just the same to me."

Patty looked at Nellie, and they both laughed.

"Andy came into the kitchen while I was cleanin up. He told me he was goin downstreet for the evenin."

Patty said, "We could ask Phyllis what's goin on. She probably knows."

"We don't need to. Let him have his privacy. He's got to go for a soldier so soon."

"Ooh," Patty said. "I hate that."

"I hate it too, but he ain't got a choice. It's the law."

"You women shouldn't talk that way. You got it all wrong. He *wants* to go. He's lookin forward to it."

"I don't care, Frank. I'm with Patty. I don't want him to go."

"Where would our country be if everybody felt that way? There's a war goin on, or ain't you noticed? People can't just pick and choose when to support their government."

"That's what Helen says. Andy's a good boy. He'll go when he has to, but right now we can let him enjoy his summer."

"I just hope that hippie girl don't try to tell him he don't have to go. Them hippies got some crazy notions."

"You don't need to worry." Nellie said, "She ain't been around lately. It's too bad for Andy. I thought he might be gettin kinda sweet on her."

Patty said, "I saw her tonight. Andy was out by her car, talkin to her."

"Maybe that explains his good mood."

"Well, I hope not. I don't want him messin around with them hippies. They're all protesters and draft dodgers. We don't want 'em around here."

"She's okay, Frank. She helped with the hay that time." Nellie didn't say it, but she liked the girl. She remembered her saying she wanted to learn country ways. Out loud, she said, "Her sister and her sister's husband are the ones that bought the old Robinson place. That makes 'em neighbors of ours."

"They've turned that farm into a commune for free love and such. That's what I've heard."

"They buy our milk. And anyway, it don't much matter. Andy's goin to be gone so soon."

"What about Phyllis then?"

"What about her? She ain't even interested in boys yet. We're goin to worry about her, but let's wait until we need to."

No one said anything to that. They sat looking out across the valley. It was almost full dark now. They watched lights winking on in the distance.

After a while Frank's voice came out of the darkness. "I remember how you tried to get *me* not to go, Ma."

"I did. I broke my heart over that one. You couldn't keep out of it. I remember you goin around fixin everythin—fences and gates, stuff that had been broke for years. I knew you was tryin to feel better about leavin me to run the place by myself. I knew you felt guilty about leavin."

"I felt guilty about everythin. I felt guilty about stayin when everybody else was already in it, and I felt guilty about leavin you to run the place by yourself."

"At least we all knew what we were fightin for. It was easy to see what it was about. Now this Vietnam thing…"

"Ma, you don't know…we got to leave it up to the people we voted for. They know more about it than we do."

"What if they're wrong? We're talkin about Andy's life here."

Patty said, "Don't talk like that, Nellie. You don't know. Frank knows more about it than we do."

"That's why I try to keep my mouth shut. I hope you're right, Frank."

"They all say it's goin to be over soon."

Nellie folded the shirt on her lap. "Well, I guess I'll go up. It's too dark to do any more mendin."

But before she had a chance to get to her feet, Patty said, "Phyllis keeps after me to take her to the pound to look for a dog. I was hopin she'd forget, but she hasn't."

"We ought to have a dog to keep the coons and such away from the chickens, and to keep the deer outa the garden. All those critters are bolder since Penny died. She was a good dog."

"All right," Patty said. "I'll do it. I'll take her to the shelter. Is that okay with you, Frank?"

"Well, I guess so. We need a dog. But you better warn Phyllis. If that dog kills chickens, we'll have to put it down. That's just the way it's gonna be. A dog is bound to be trouble. It might chase the cows or bark at the milk customers."

"It'll give Phyllis somethin to do all summer. That's got to be good."

"All right. I can't argue with both of you at once. Just make sure Phyllis is ready to do a lot of trainin."

"I'll tell her," Patty said. "She's gonna be so excited."

Nellie stood up slowly. "Well, I'll see you." She picked up the sewing basket and went inside, leaving the two of them sitting in silence, looking out at the night sky and the rain.

CHAPTER 10

After supper Andy changed clothes and went down to the kitchen. Gram was there alone.

"I'm gonna hitch into town, if anybody wants to know," he said.

Gram stopped washing dishes and turned off the water. She looked him up and down. "Really? You're gonna get wet...in your good clothes."

"I don't care. I got some friends to meet." He hoped she noticed that he said he was meeting more than one person.

"That's nice, honey." She turned the water back on without saying any more.

Andy went outside and started down the hill. There was no sign of Phyllis. Maybe the rain was keeping her from following him.

When he got around the last bend in the road, he saw Crystal's little black Volkswagen below. He hurried the rest of the way and opened the door.

"You got here first."

"See," she said. "You're all wet. I knew I should have picked you up by your house."

"Do you care if I get your seat wet?"

"Not a bit."

He got in, and she wheeled around and headed toward Severance.

He didn't know where they were going. He had only planned as far as their meeting. He was trying to think of something to offer her when she turned into the parking lot of the Texas Café.

"What're you stoppin here for?" he said.

"I thought we could get some coffee or maybe ice cream. Do you want something to eat?"

"Not here. All my dad's friends hang out in the Texas."

"So?"

"If they see us together, they'll call him up to tell him about it."

"Doesn't he know about me?"

"I don't think so."

She looked at him steadily for so long it made him uncomfortable. Did it hurt her feelings that he hadn't told anybody about her?

Then she said, "I haven't told anybody about you either, not even my sister. I guess it's our secret, isn't it?" She put the car in gear and drove out of the parking lot, heading toward town.

But where were they going? He had invited her. It was a date in a way. "Would you like to go to the movies?" he said.

"I don't know. I guess it depends on what the movie is."

"Keep on straight through the middle of town, and we can see."

It was *The Sound of Music*. "Oh no," she said. "I don't think so. You don't want to see it, do you?"

"No thanks," he said. He was relieved, because he didn't know whether he was supposed to pay for her ticket or not.

They couldn't keep driving around, and he didn't feel comfortable telling her where all the kids went to park, so he told her to drive to the feed store. The parking lot looked out over the river.

It was dusk-dark. The river was misty, blurred by the rain. Their car was the only one in the parking lot. Her beautiful face was turned toward him, so that one side was shining in the light from the streetlamp. He longed to kiss her, but should he? He hesitated. The other evening in the woods, he didn't think about it, he just did it, pushed by the thought that it didn't matter because he would never see her again. Now there were possibilities, and that made him cautious.

She looked into his face seriously. "Do you have a girlfriend?"

"You mean now?"

"I just wondered."

"I had a girlfriend last year, but we broke up."

"Why?"

"I don't know. It wasn't workin. She lived on the other side of West Severance, and I didn't have a car."

"I'm sorry," she said. She traced a line down the side of his face with her finger. "No, I'm not sorry."

He kissed her then, but it wasn't much of a kiss. They couldn't get close to each other because of the bucket seats and the gear shift.

She sat back, still looking at him. "What was her name?"

"What?" He couldn't understand her question.

"Your girlfriend's name."

"Oh...Sandra."

Her eyes were exploring his face. "Does Sandra know you are going to war?"

"I don't know...we never talked about it...but everybody..."

"Maybe Sandra didn't want to fall in love with someone who was going away so soon, someone who might get killed."

"I don't think she..." He stopped in confusion. Was Crystal thinking about her own situation? He didn't know how to ask her what she meant, without sounding like he thought she might be saying she could fall in love with him. So, he kissed her instead.

Then he said, "It wasn't like that. I think I ended it by not asking her to go to the prom. I knew she wanted to."

"Did you take somebody else?"

"No...I just didn't go." He couldn't explain that he didn't want to put his parents to the expense of buying him a new suit when he would be going into the army so soon and maybe not coming home again. "What about you? You probably have lots of boyfriends, don't you?"

"No. I don't. There wasn't anybody at my school...none of them knew how to do things...not like you. It was obvious when I saw their hands. They were soft and clean and unmarked. They were girlish." She picked up one of his hands and looked at it. "It's easy to see that you know how to work." She smiled at him. "I want you to teach me the things you know how to do."

He said, "I wish there was some place we could go to be together."

"Me too. It was wonderful the other night in the woods. I wish..."

"It wouldn't be like that tonight...not in the rain."

"What can we do?"

"I don't know," he said.

"I want you to teach me about the woods. We could meet there... when it's not raining."

"What we need is a place to go when it is rainin."

"What would you do if you were living in the woods?"

"I'd have a camp with a shelter of some kind and a place to build a fire."

"Andy, we could build a camp like that! Oh, let's do it! Could we?"

"Where?"

"Up there between your house and mine."

"That's not very far away."

"What difference does that make?"

"We don't want them to see our fire. If my dad thought there was a fire in the woods, he'd be right up there to check it out. We don't want *that* to happen."

"What shall we do, then?"

"Let's look around in the daylight. Maybe we can find a spot."

"Oh, this is so exciting! Let's start tomorrow."

"I should be able to get away in the late morning, say by eleven. The rain might be over. We don't have any hay down, so I won't have to help Pop. I can bring some tools."

In the middle of the night, he was suddenly wide-awake. His clock said ten past two. He lay in bed trying to remember all the things he wanted to take and worrying about how he was going to get all of it across the back field and into the woods without anyone seeing him.

He got up and opened the door. The house was so quiet that he could hear the ticking of the big clock in the kitchen. He got dressed and went silently down the stairs.

He tiptoed around, gathering what he needed, using a flashlight instead of the house lights. After about an hour, he had a big pile in the shed—an ax and a buck saw, the blanket from his bed. He got Pop's big canvas tarp, which Pop hardly ever used, and some matches and a small roll of baler twine.

It was all up there before daylight, but it was slow. He had to go along the tree line on the edge of the field. It was still raining, and very dark, but he couldn't take the chance that someone in the house would get up to go to the bathroom and see him going up the back field.

Still, he managed to do what he needed to do. He went back to his room and took off his wet clothes and lay down on his bed to wait until it was time to milk.

He got to their meeting place before eleven, and even though it was still very wet, he sat down under the apple tree where he could see the back of Crystal's house and the field below the woods.

The next thing he knew, he was dreaming that Rosie stepped on his foot. He opened his eyes. Crystal was standing there.

"You look so cute when you're asleep. You were snoring too. Did you know that? But I didn't mean to wake you up."

He was embarrassed to have her see him like that. He jumped to his feet.

"Don't get up. I was going to sit down beside you. I didn't mean to bump your foot."

"I dreamed Rosie stepped on it."

"The cow? That must have hurt."

"In my dream it didn't hurt, and I wondered why."

"I love the way dreams change ordinary life."

"I was waitin for you."

"I know. It's only a little while after eleven. I'm not that late."

"It's fine," he said. "I want to show you the place I found for our camp."

"Did you get the stuff you were going to bring, the tools and stuff?"

"It's already at the campsite."

He started up the logging road. "Come on."

She hurried to catch up, and then she slipped her hand into his, and they walked up the hill side by side.

Not far from the trail on the Keyeses' side of the hill was the spot he had chosen for the camp. It was in a little hollow. He walked over to it. "Come here," he said. "What do you think? Do you like it?"

She took a few slow steps. "Here?"

"You don't like it." He was disappointed.

She took a few more steps. "No, it isn't that. I just can't picture it." She was clearly puzzled.

He tried to explain why he chose this spot. "We have to have a place where we can have a fire they won't see from the house. Down in this little hollow, the fire won't show. That gives us some privacy." He could feel the package of condoms in his pocket. He wanted to see if she understood what he meant by privacy, but he didn't dare look at her. Last night she had wanted it as much as he did, but today might be different.

She looked around. He couldn't tell what she was thinking. Then she smiled at him. "Okay, you know best. Tell me what to do."

He cut a lot of spruce boughs, and they dragged them to the camp, where they stacked them in a springy pile and covered them with the tarp. Andy tied some of the twine between two small maples so they could drape the other end of the tarp over it. It made a rough tent to protect the bed from the rain. He staked the corners with small pieces of wood that he pounded into the ground and tied to the tarp with twine. They moved a lot of rocks and dug a little pit for a fire.

It took most of the afternoon, and they both got sweaty and dirty, but by the time he had to leave to go milk, they had a place of their own. They were eager to try it out, so they arranged to meet in the evening at the edge of the woods on Crystal's side of the hill.

Andy hurried through his work and supper and cleaning up, but when he got to the meeting place, he found a note from Crystal stuck on a branch. The note said she couldn't meet him tonight, and that she would explain when she saw him. Disappointed, he went up the trail to the camp and tried to make a few improvements, but his heart wasn't in it, and he went home.

He was hoping he could slip into the house without anyone seeing him, but when he got closer, he saw that everyone was standing outside by Pop's truck. They all looked at him. No one seemed to notice that he'd just come out of the woods in his town clothes.

Phyllis called him to come see, so he had to go over to them. Ma and Pop and Gram were looking down at Phyllis, who was kneeling beside a little brown and white dog. He had forgotten that today was the day they were going to the pound. The dog was crouched in the driveway. It looked up at Andy out of the tops of its eyes with a hunted expression. It was trembling.

Phyllis patted it. "She's so beautiful. I'm goin to name her Moxie."

Andy said, "That dog looks scared to death."

"She'll get over it. We'll teach her that she's safe here. Won't we, Moxie?" She stroked the dog some more.

The dog sat there shaking. She looked like she would run and hide someplace, if she just knew which way to go.

Gram said, "What do you think of her, Andy?"

"She don't look like much of a guard dog."

"Give her a little time. This ain't her place yet. She'll be different when she feels at home here."

"What kind is she?"

"Mostly beagle with maybe a little shepherd in there. That's what they said at the pound."

"Is she goin to get bigger?"

Phyllis looked up at him. "She's fully grown, Andy. She's already six years old. She's just the right size, ain't you, Moxie? Don't listen to him."

"I just wondered, is all."

"Can she sleep in my room with me, Ma? She won't be so scared if she's with me. Will you, Moxie dear?"

"She's got to stay outside, Phyllis. That's the rule."

"But, Ma, she might run away. She don't know she's supposed to live here."

"Pop can get a rope and tie her. Then she'll have to stay. She can be on the porch."

"Oh Ma, she'll get cold."

"You can put a box out with some hay in it. That'll do for a bed for her. She can have some food and water too. She can't come in, that's all."

That broke up the group. Ma and Gram went into the house, and Pop went to get a rope from the barn.

"I could sneak her in when they're gone to bed," Phyllis said. She looked at Andy. He could tell she was beginning to wonder why he had his town clothes on. He didn't want her to start asking questions.

"Sneak her in. I won't tell on you," he said, and he walked away before she could ask him why he was dressed the way he was.

The next day he went up to the place where Crystal left the note, hoping to find her, or at least to find another note. He didn't want to miss her, so he went up in the morning and again in the afternoon, but there was no word from her. He decided to get the milking out of the way, and then go to their camp. He could make a fire. Maybe she would show up.

He had just started to milk when Phyllis appeared in the doorway with Moxie on a leash made of baling twine.

"What are you doin milkin so early?"

"Nothin. I just thought I'd get it done. What's wrong with that?"

"Nothin. But Andy, I got somethin to tell you. You ain't goin to believe it."

He looked around at her. "What is it?"

She stepped into the milking room and stood beside Rosie's back end. Moxie stayed in the doorway at the end of the leash.

Phyllis was almost whispering. "I took Moxie for a walk in the woods, and you won't believe what I found."

"What?" he said. He was milking again.

"Somebody's campin up there. They built a lean-to and a firepit. They got a tarp just like Pop's big one for a tent. I don't think they've been there very long because they ain't had a fire yet."

Andy kept on milking. This was something he hadn't foreseen.

"We've got to tell Pop. They could be robbers or murderers. It makes me scared just to think about it."

It was because of the dog. Phyllis never went up in the woods by herself. Andy tried to stay calm. "It's too soon to get Pop into it, Phyllis. We don't know. He might of told 'em it would be okay. I'll go up there tonight and take a look. Maybe I'll leave 'em a note."

"Okay. Moxie and I can come with you."

"You better not. We don't want Moxie to get scared or hurt or nothin."

"But what about you?"

"I can take care of myself in the woods. You and Moxie stay down here, and don't say nothin to Ma and Pop or Gram until I check it out."

"Okay, Andy, if you say so." Then she looked puzzled. "Don't you want me to tell you where it's at?"

"Oh right…sure. Is it hard to find?"

"No, it's easy. It's near the trail that goes straight up from the back pasture, the one you were workin on a while ago. I was takin Moxie up there to show her where her property ends. It's right before you get to the stone wall at the top."

"Okay, Phyllis, I'll check it out, and then we can decide what to do."

"Thanks, Andy, I'm glad I told you." She went out the door. "Come on, Moxie. I want to brush you."

He hadn't been thinking clearly. It was crazy to build the camp on the Keyes side of the hill. He bet no one living on the Robinson place ever went in the woods. They wouldn't know whether there was a camp there or not. He was just lucky Phyllis didn't find the camp when he and Crystal were in it.

He'd have to move it right away, before Phyllis started snooping around again. He could dismantle the lean-to and move everything over to the other side of the hill and pile it someplace until he could find a good spot for a new camp. Phyllis wouldn't go into the Robinson woods. He should have thought of that in the first place.

CHAPTER 11

Nellie was just heading out to the garden when the phone rang. It was Ginny Alvarez from down the road, asking her to come as quick as she could. Al cut himself with his ax. Nellie said she'd be right over.

She found Frank mending a gate in the barn and told him she had to take the truck. She grabbed her nurse's bag and a couple of pillows and took off her apron.

She was just arranging the pillows on the truck seat so she could reach the pedals, when Phyllis happened along with Moxie on a string.

"Where you goin, Gram? Can I come with you?"

"No, you can't. I'm just goin down to the Alvarezes'. Al's hurt."

"I could drive you. I can reach the pedals better 'n you can."

"I need you to stay here. There's a load of laundry in the washin machine. Get it out when it's done and hang it on the line."

"But I want to go with you."

"I need you here. I'll see you later."

"Oh shoot!"

"Be good now." She put the truck in gear and started down the hill.

When she got to the Alvarezes', she went to their back door. It was open. The steps were a couple of wobbly cinder blocks on the dirt floor of the garage. She had to set her bag down and use her hands to get up into the kitchen. Al was across the room, sitting at the table with his back to the door.

"It's Nellie, Al. Come to take care of you."

He turned partway around. "Thank you, Nellie. I need some fixin all right. Come see what I done."

He was a big man. His heavy leg in its workboot was propped on a kitchen chair. There was a pool of blood on the linoleum floor below it.

Nellie set her bag on the table. "Where's Ginny at?"

"She was here a minute ago. She's around somewheres."

"All right. I'm goin to go ahead and cut your pants. I'll cut up the seam so she can put 'em back together. She'll have to mend the hole you made anyhow."

Ginny came in while she was cutting open the pants leg.

"You got here quick, Nellie. I appreciate it."

"It was luck I answered the phone before I went outdoors." She laid back the cloth. "Okay, let's see what we got here."

It was a deep wound into the thick muscle of Al's calf. "I guess it's good you missed the bone," Nellie said. They all three looked at the cut. It ran diagonally across Al's lower leg.

"I put some tobacco in there to stop the blood," he said.

"I see that. I'll have to take the tobacco out if I want to close it good. It's nice and straight anyhow. If you went to the hospital, they could give you somethin before they sewed it. It might heal up better."

"No, damn it, Nellie. I ain't goin to no hospital. They'd take my money, and they wouldn't do half as good as you."

"You'll have a scar if I do it."

"I don't care. Clean it up and put it together so I can get back to work. I don't intend to sit around all day."

Nellie and Ginny looked at each other and laughed. "Okay Al, I'll put some stitches in it. Do you have any whiskey?"

"I wish I did. Just do it. I can take it."

"Okay. I'll do my best. Ginny, I'll need a basin of water, some soap and a clean cloth."

Ginny set everything on the table, and Nellie started to work. When she swabbed the wound to take out the tobacco and clean it, Al groaned and shifted around.

"Sit still, Al. I can't do a decent job if you keep movin like that."

"It hurts somethin wicked, Nellie."

"Too bad you don't have a little whiskey. It'd come in handy about now."

The wound began to bleed again as she worked. She had to keep patting it dry, so she could see what she was doing. When she started taking stitches, Al couldn't stop moving around. Still, she managed to get five in along the length of it before she had to give up. It was bleeding more now, oozing out between the stitches. She covered the whole thing with gauze pads and held them in place with adhesive tape. Ginny watched everything she did.

"You're goin to have to change these pads whenever the blood soaks through, Ginny. I'll leave you a supply of 'em and some tape."

Al said, "Thanks, Nellie. It feels good now that you ain't pokin at it no more."

"I hope you'll sit around for at least a couple of hours and give it a chance to stop bleedin."

"I don't know how long I can wait. I got stuff to do."

"Well, do the best you can. Maybe Ginny can keep you down." She packed up her bag and went home.

At supper Frank wanted to hear all about it.

"I put in five stitches before I had to quit. If Al had had some whiskey, I might of got in a few more, but it was a nice, straight cut, so it went together pretty well. I called over there a little while ago. Ginny said he was good. He sat at the kitchen table with his leg propped up and sharpened his axes and his saw."

After the dishes were done, Nellie took off her apron and went into the living room. She wanted to talk to Frank about the garden, but he was watching the television news, so she picked up the shirt she was mending and sat down to wait for a commercial break.

She couldn't have made Frank hear her anyway, because the television was so loud. There was a battle in the jungle. They were all running and shouting and shooting. Helicopters landed to pick up bloody soldiers, and every one of those boys looked like Andy.

Nellie couldn't watch. She said, "I don't know how you can look at that stuff, knowin that Andy's goin to be in it so soon."

"*I* had to go to war. Now it's his turn."

"Frank, it's different. You chose to go. Andy ain't got a choice. If only he was goin to college...them boys don't have to go."

"What would Andy want to go to college for?"

"I don't know."

"Besides, we ain't got that kinda money."

"Well, it's not fair."

"There's nothin new about that. And you and I ain't goin to change it. Anyway, Andy wants to go for a soldier."

"He figures he might as well like it, since he ain't got a choice."

"It'll make a man of him."

"If it don't maim him or kill him."

"You let *me* go, Ma."

"I didn't want to, but at least I could see the point of it. This one's so far away, and nobody can't say what it's about."

"That ain't true. It's a war to fight the commonists. If they get control of Vietnam, the next thing we know, they'll be over here. We can't have that. They want to take our country. The people who run our governmint think we need to fight, and they know a lot more about it than you do. Even Senator Aiken thinks we ought to keep some soldiers in Vietnam."

"Well, if Andy…"

"Ma, you got enough work to do. You don't need to be messin in this business when you don't know nothin about it. Leave it to the governmint. They know what to do. Take care of your work, and let them in the governmint take care of theirs."

Nellie sighed and looked down at the shirt in her lap, the one she was supposed to be mending.

The next time a commercial came on, she said, "Okay, Frank. This is my business—the deer have been gettin in the garden. They trampled some corn last night and ate some spinach. This is the first time they've trashed anythin, but I've been seein signs. It's past time now to stop 'em."

"We didn't have much trouble last year."

"Penny took care of it. The deer knew better than to come down close to the house when Penny was around."

"We could put Phyllis's new dog out there."

"We'd have to tie her so she didn't run off. The deer might get the idea that they didn't need to worry about her, and she might get the idea that she didn't need to guard her new home."

There was a news story about people rioting. Frank saw that she was watching it. He went over to the television and turned it off. "I don't care about the rest of the news. I just wanted to see what was happenin in the war."

Nellie started to say that rioting in Buffalo was a war too, and one that was going on in our country. That made it more important than something that was taking place on the other side of the world. But she didn't want to start an argument, and what was happening to the garden was the most important of all, so she said, "What can we do about the deer? We got to do somethin."

"Suppose I put a floodlight on the back of the house? When we hear 'em out there, we flip it on. I can get a shot off before they can run." He was grinning at her. "If we don't have any spinach, we can eat venison instead. What about that?"

She had to laugh. He looked like he did when he was a little kid. She said, "They'll be back tonight. I'm sure of it."

"It won't take much to set up a light. I can probably have it ready by dark. How's that?"

Nellie stood in the doorway and watched while Frank rigged the floodlight under the eaves of the house. In the twilight field above the garden, she could see Andy heading toward the woods. When he looked down at the house and saw his dad on the ladder, he changed directions and slipped into the shadows on the west side of the field.

Frank didn't see him. He came down the ladder and said, "I'm goin to run this cord in through the window. If it works, I can make a switch for it right by the back door, so I can flip it on and step out with my deer rifle. But for tonight, we'll just plug it in. Okay, Ma?"

"Thanks, Frank. I'll test the light, while you put away the ladder." Frank didn't notice anything odd about what she said. He was in a hurry to get the ladder put away before full dark.

She wanted to give Andy a few minutes to take cover before she lit up the back field. She was pretty sure she knew what he was doing up there. She'd been in the woods looking for mushrooms when she found the camp he made. She understood why he was so eager for a place where he could have a little privacy. She remembered her own young days when she and Phil first got together and the most important thing in the world was to find some place where they could be alone, not just for sex, although there was plenty of that, but also to be with each other. There seemed to be so many things to say in those early days, even though she couldn't remember now what they talked about. What she remembered was the endless pleasure of being together. He died so young that she would never know if that would have lasted. And Andy had so little time before he had to go to war. Nellie wasn't going to say anything to anyone, but she planned to do all she could to get him chances to spend that time with the hippie girl.

When she thought Andy was safely out of sight, she plugged in the light and saw the garden and some of the field blaze up a bright green. Frank came back, and they agreed it just might work to deter the deer. Frank got his rifle and stood it ready by the back door. He said, "I'm goin to shoot it off tomorrow anyhow for the Fourth."

CHAPTER 12

Maymay was sitting at the kitchen table. She jumped up when Cynthia came into the room.

"Oh, come here, my dear. Let me give you a kiss, and then I'll get you a cup of coffee. Where's Laura?"

"She's dressing Orion. They'll be down in a minute."

Maymay put a cup of coffee down on the table. "Sit down, Cynthia. Do you want some cream?"

"I can get it, Maymay. I don't want you to wait on me. You have enough to worry about."

Cynthia got out the pitcher of cream and poured some into her coffee. She could hear Laura coming down the stairs, so she left the cream on the table for her.

When Cynthia asked what the doctor said about Papa, she saw a shadow pass over Maymay's face before she answered. "The doctor said he would be fine. He *did* have a heart attack, but it didn't damage his heart, thank goodness."

By this time Laura and Orion were sitting at the table too. Orion was on Laura's lap. She had laid out a row of cheerios, and he was carefully picking them up one by one and putting them into his mouth.

"When do you think Papa can come home?"

Maymay sighed. "It's going to be a long time. He has to get his strength back. He might have to go to one of those rehabilitation places. It could be months, but the important thing is that he's going to get better."

"Maymay, you don't have to get breakfast for us. We can get something on the way home."

"But I want to. I'm going to make you some bacon and eggs. Can the baby eat eggs?"

"He loves them."

"Well then, I'll make him some too."

"But don't you need to get to the hospital to be with Papa?"

"He's all right. I talked to him on the phone this morning. I'll be there in time to have some lunch with him. How long will it take you girls to get back to Laura's house?"

Cynthia looked at Laura. She couldn't remember how long it took them on the way down. It was night. Orion was cross. They were both so worried that Papa was going to die before they got there to say goodbye. And Cynthia had her own private worries about whether Andy would find the note, and even if he did, what would he think? He might think she was standing him up.

Laura said, "Don't worry about us, Maymay. It takes less than five hours. We'll be home sometime in the middle of the afternoon."

"I'm so glad you girls came down. I loved seeing you and the sweet baby, and I think Papa appreciated that you worried about him enough to make the long journey."

"Everyone loves Papa. We came as fast as we could when we heard he was in the hospital. We're so grateful that he's going to be all right."

Laura said, "We'll come back and visit during the summer. Maybe he'll be home by then. Paul can come with us. He would have come this time, but we left in such a hurry."

They didn't get on the road until almost eleven. They wanted to leave everything in order for Maymay, so they did the dishes and changed the sheets, even though she said they didn't need to.

When they drove out the driveway, she was standing on the porch, waving goodbye.

Cynthia said, "She looks so small and fragile standing there. I hope she'll be all right. The next few months are going to be hard for her. I hope Mom can help her."

"Did you notice that she never said Orion's name?"

"Maybe she couldn't remember it."

"Oh no, it wasn't that. She thought I shouldn't have given him such a hippie name."

"You don't know that."

"Mom told me."

"Yeah, but Mom is much more likely to think that way than Maymay is. She could've just said it to make you think the whole family was on her side."

"There's lots I could say about that." Laura sighed. "But listen, Cynthia, I've got to get gas soon, and then let's keep going until Orion gets cross."

"That's fine with me."

"When Orion gets hungry, we can trade drivers."

That's what they did. It was an easy trip, and they made good time. Cynthia tried not to speculate about Andy. She tried to watch the countryside going by, but since a lot of their trip was on the new interstate, there wasn't that much to see. The sky was overcast, but the roads were dry. It was warm and muggy. Still, Orion was good, and they got home even earlier than Laura thought they would.

Cynthia helped Laura unload the car. There was a folding crib and a little chair for Orion, and all his clothes and diapers. She and Laura each had an overnight bag, and they had the groceries that they bought on the way. It took a while to get it all into the house.

Paul wasn't home, and Laura was busy getting Orion settled, so Cynthia had a good chance to go up to the top of the back field to see if Andy got her note or left one for her.

She found the tree where they met. Her heart beat fast. She realized that part of her believed she would find him sleeping there, the way she had before. But of course, he wasn't there, and there was no note either. She looked in all the low branches, and in the grass and weeds below the tree. Then she looked all around in a circle farther off in case the wind had blown away her note or his reply. There was nothing. She felt like crying. She had been so sure there would be some sign from him.

Then she remembered the camp. Of course, if he had left her a message, it would be in the little lean-to they had built together. She started up the road, which was really just two faint dirt tracks with a row of grassy weeds between them. The light was dim and green. Andy had no idea that she was afraid to be in the woods alone. She would go up to their camp, and she would make sure he never found out that it was hard for her.

So it was a triumph when she got to the stone wall. She had been tempted to turn back several times, but she had persisted. She knew the camp wasn't far from the top on Andy's side. She went down slowly, looking off through the woods, sure she would be able to spot the little canvas shelter. She kept walking along and looking, until she was certain she had gone too far. She began to think she might have remembered it wrong, so she walked back to the top studying the other side of the trail.

After a couple of trips, when she was almost in tears, she decided to go off the trail as far as she thought their camp was and walk down the hill parallel to the trail.

When she did that, she saw the circle of stones they had made for a fire pit, and then she spotted the flattened ground under the trees where the lean-to had been. The reason she hadn't seen the camp before was because the camp was gone.

She sat down on a rock and looked around. The camp had been here. She could see that. Why would he have taken it down? She looked for a note that would explain it, but there wasn't one. Maybe he was so angry when she left that he didn't want to see her anymore.

He hadn't changed anything in his life for her. *She* was the one who had changed what she was doing so they could be together. It was all a big mistake. She sat there in the alien forest and cried.

After a while she walked down the hill, wishing she had gone to San Francisco with Bob. She was going to miss all the fun of the Summer of Love because of Andy. The future stretched out in front of her, and it was a blank.

If she wanted to find out what was going on with Andy, she would have to go to the Keyes farm at milking time. She found Laura upstairs, trying to put Orion down for a nap.

"Laura, I can't believe I left my toothbrush at Maymay's. I have to go to the drugstore and get one. Do you need anything?"

"Oh Cynthy, I'm sorry. We could have stopped when we went through town."

"But I didn't know until we got home." She didn't want to lie to Laura, but she needed a reason to leave when they just got home, and she didn't want to say anything about Andy yet.

She drove into Severance, and when she thought it was getting close to the time when Andy had to milk, she started out of town toward the Keyes farm. A few miles out of town, there he was, hitchhiking. He dropped his arm in surprise when he saw who was slowing down to pick him up.

Was that because he didn't want to see her again? She couldn't tell, but she wasn't going to take no for an answer. He needed a ride, and she needed to explain to him why she had to leave so abruptly.

As soon as he opened the door, she said, "So, we meet again."

"Can I get in?"

"Are you mad at me? I was afraid you'd be mad at me for spoiling our plans. Did you get my note?"

"I didn't know what happened."

"My Papa, my grandfather, had a heart attack. Laura and I drove down to the hospital. He lives in Hartford. We left in a hurry. We thought he was going to die."

"Oh, I didn't know."

"Did you get my note?"

"Yes, but it didn't…"

"I had to write it so fast, and I didn't know what was going to happen."

"What did happen?"

"The doctor says he'll be okay, but it's going to take him a long time to recover."

"When did you get back?"

"Just a couple of hours ago. I went up to the tree—our tree—to see if you left me a note, and then I went up to see if you left one at our camp, but the camp was gone. Then I *really* thought you were mad at me. Are you?"

"No, not at all."

Her hand was resting on the gear shift. He covered it with his own hand. She wanted to stop the car so she could look at him, but she knew he had to get home soon.

"Phyllis found the camp. She was goin to tell Pop, because she had this idea that it was made by robbers."

"Robbers?"

"It's okay. I told her not to tell nobody until I checked it out. I told her I was goin to go up there and talk to them and leave them a note. Then I took everythin down and told her they were gone."

"But now we don't have anywhere to go, do we?"

"I started us another camp. It ain't as nice. I ain't done much yet. We'll have to work on it. But this time, it's on your side of the hill. Nobody won't have any reason to be in those woods until huntin season. Your sister and brother-in-law probably won't go up there, will they?"

"No, I don't think they'd have any reason to."

"Phyllis never goes up in the woods by herself. She wouldn't of found it, except that she has this new dog, and she wanted to show her around the property or somethin. She won't go on the Robinson land."

"I'm so glad that's what happened. I really thought you didn't want to have anything to do with me anymore."

"How could you think that?"

"Because I stood you up—or I thought you would think I did."

"I couldn't put a note at the old camp sayin I'd moved it. Who knows when Phyllis might be snoopin around…but I never thought you would think I was mad at you."

When they got to the bottom of the Keyeses' road, Cynthia pulled over. "What now?" she said.

He squeezed her hand before he took his away. He opened the door. "Let's pick up where we left off. I have to go milk, but I could meet you here at…would seven work for you?"

"Oh yes, I'll make it work." She drove away without even looking back. She was thinking about tonight.

CHAPTER 13

When Andy finished milking, he put Rosie out in the night pasture with the others and took the milk up to the house. He was hoping the kitchen would be empty. It would give him a chance to grab a few things for the new camp.

But Gram was there, standing at the stove, frying onions. Andy was hungry, and they smelled awful good, but he wasn't going to have any, not tonight. He didn't want to take a chance on his breath smelling like onions. He would have to pass them up.

She smiled at him.

He stood there for a minute watching her move the onions around in the pan. Then he said, "I'm goin to get drafted pretty soon now."

"Oh honey, I know that."

"Well, what do you think about it?"

She looked at him, not smiling any more. "I don't like it," she said.

"But do you think I ought to go fight in that war?"

She stirred the onions, and then she sighed and looked around at the kitchen door. "Andy, you probably ought to talk to your dad. He's the one watches the television news every night. I don't know nothin. It's too far away for me to understand."

"I know what he thinks, Gram. He says we have to stop the commonists. But I don't see how they could get over here, even if they wanted to."

"I guess you been talkin to that hippie girl about it."

He could feel the red spreading up his face. He nodded. "She says our country shouldn't be fightin like that on the other side of the world."

"You got to figure it out for yourself, Andy, but I can tell you that the whole thing don't make sense to me. Think of all it costs. We could be usin that money for our own people. There's so many that need help."

"But what should *I* do, Gram? All my friends are out there already. Should I just leave 'em in danger and not go to be with 'em? Maybe I could help. What if my friends need me? What if my country does?"

That was when Phyllis and Pop walked into the kitchen together. Gram gave Andy a quick smile. He knew that meant their conversation was over.

"I'll be in my room," he said as he went out. When he got upstairs, he saw that the bathroom was empty. He was able to take a shower and wash his hair. He even shaved, although he didn't need to.

He thought about the war. It got more and more confusing. There were arguments on both sides. He might lose Crystal if he signed up to go when they called him. But if he didn't, he could miss out on the most important part of his life. He might have a chance to be a hero, like Pop was when he was young.

Suppose he did what Crystal wanted him to do, and then it didn't work out with her? The war could be over before he got to be in it. All his friends would come home with stories of what they'd seen and done, and he would have nothing.

By the time he was dressed, Phyllis was standing in the door of his room. "Gram says come to supper...hey, how come you got your good clothes on?"

"If it's any of your business, which it ain't, I'm goin into town after."

"Do Ma and Pop know?"

"You can tell 'em if you want to. They don't care. I'm old enough."

"Are you goin to the fireworks?"

"I might, if they have 'em."

"Well, come down now," she said. "Gram told me to tell you."

At supper Andy hoped that someone, maybe Gram, would bring up the subject of the war, but no one did, and he didn't know how to start the conversation without letting everyone know he was changing his mind about signing on to be a soldier.

When everyone was getting up from the table, he said, "I'm goin to hitch into town to see if they have the fireworks, if that's all right."

No one said anything. He took that for permission. He got his jeans jacket off the hook by the door and went out. The rain hadn't started yet, but it was about to. He could smell the water in the air. Maybe they wouldn't have the fireworks after all.

She pulled up just as he got to the bottom of the hill. He opened the door and slid in.

She said, "Where do you think we should go?"

"We can't go to the new camp tonight because I ain't had time to build us a shelter."

"We don't need a shelter. It's warm out."

"That's because it's just about to start rainin."

"How do you know that?" And just then some drops splashed onto the windshield.

They both laughed.

"That's amazing. One more thing I want you to teach me." She put the car in gear. "I guess we have to drive around again, wishing for a place to go."

Now he was sorry he hadn't done more. "I would of worked harder on the new camp, but I didn't know if you was goin to come back. It seemed like it might be a waste of time."

She said, "I guess I'll drive to that feed store, and we can park by the river again."

"Okay," he said. "We can work on the new camp tomorrow."

She parked the car where they had parked before. There was no one around tonight either. That was probably because of the rain.

She leaned toward him, looking into his eyes. "I wish I hadn't had to leave to see my granddad. You know I had to go, don't you? I mean, it would have been terrible if he'd died, and I hadn't even gone down to see him. Besides, Laura had to have someone to help her with Orion. But I'm so sad I had to leave like that, and now our camp is gone."

"It's good it happened the way it did. What if Phyllis found the camp when we were there? But we need to work on it right away. We don't have much time to be together."

She put her arms around his neck, and he kissed her. Then she leaned back, a little out of breath, and said, "What do you mean we don't have much time? I know I have to go back to school in September, but I'll be able to come up for weekends, and you can come and see me down there too."

"Yeah, but I'm not goin to be here after September. I'll be drafted by then."

She pulled back farther and looked into his face. "Are you really going to let that happen? I don't believe it."

"Oh, you can believe it all right. And it's worse than just gettin drafted. I'm goin to get sent straight to Vietnam."

"But Andy, don't..."

"I have no choice."

"But you could get hurt."

He shrugged.

"Or worse."

He shrugged again.

She said, "We can find a way out of it."

He laughed. "Let's not waste the time we've got." He kissed her. "My friends are already there."

"But, Andy, it's wrong, and anyway, I don't want you to get killed."

"Lots of people are gettin killed."

"Lots of people are protesting against the war too."

He shrugged. "I don't know...our governmint says it's what we need to do."

"You don't believe that, do you?"

"My dad thinks we have to fight the commonists. He was in the war in Europe, and he pays attention to the news and all that. He thinks it's important that I go. I've heard him arguing with Ma and Gram about it."

"What do they say?"

"They don't want me to go because I might get hurt. I don't know what they think about the war."

"It's wrong." She pulled back and looked him in the face. "People on both sides are getting killed for no reason, just because Johnson doesn't have the guts to say it's wrong and get our soldiers out of there. If you go, you'll be making it worse, and anyway, what about us?"

"We've got until September."

"I have to go back to school in September."

"See, it's all gonna work out."

"But Andy…"

He interrupted what she was going to say by kissing her again.

After a minute she pulled away. She ran her finger down his cheek and said, "I have until September to convince you not to go. I'm sure by then I can make you see how wrong it is. I don't want to lose you."

He didn't want to talk about it anymore. It was something that was going to happen in the future, and what was happening now was what interested him. He kissed her again, and then he said, "What we need to do is plan about tomorrow. Let's meet to work on the camp."

CHAPTER 14

As soon as everyone was finished with breakfast, Nellie grabbed a hat and her picking bag and headed out to the garden. She didn't even wait to put the dishes in the sink. It was a still morning, sparkling in the freshly washed sunshine. She had just started picking peas when Phyllis showed up.

"I been lookin everywhere for you, Gram. Are you all right?"

"I'm fine...why?" She looked down the row of peas to where Phyllis was standing at the edge of the garden. She had Moxie on a string.

"The breakfast ain't been cleaned up. I thought maybe somethin was wrong."

"I can clean up later. I wanted to see if the deer got into the garden last night, and I wanted to pick peas before it got too hot."

"Okay. Was there any deer tracks?"

"It don't look like they were here, but I need to do more checkin around."

"We'll do it. Come on, Moxie. Start sniffin." They walked along slowly with Phyllis studying the ground.

Moxie didn't pay much attention, but she looked a lot better than she did when she first arrived. She wasn't cringing all the time. Sometimes she was even able to take an interest in her surroundings. When they completed the circuit of the garden, they stopped at the end of the row of peas.

Nellie looked down the row at them. "Phyllis, where'd Moxie get that collar?"

"I made it for her. She needed a collar."

"It looks like leather. Tell me you found it with the old horse harness in the barn, and that your dad said you could have it."

"Well, not exactly." She moved a few steps to the side, so that Nellie couldn't look directly at her. "I tried to find some harness that would work, but it was all so old and dirty. Moxie didn't like it."

"So where'd you get that collar then?"

"I made it. It used to be my belt, but I didn't need it. My pants stay up just fine with a safety pin." She stepped over a few steps and pulled up her shirt so Nellie could see.

"Phyllis, that ain't the whole story. That belt must have been much too big for Moxie."

"I fixed it. It was easy. I put in some new holes and cut off the extra."

Nellie had to turn toward the peas, so Phyllis wouldn't see that she was smiling. "Your Ma's goin to skin you for ruinin your belt like you done."

"She might not notice. She don't pay much attention to Moxie."

"I won't say nothin, but she's bound to notice sooner or later."

"I know. But Moxie had to have a collar. I couldn't train her without she had a collar on."

"It's done now. Keep lookin to see if the deer were here. I can't believe they left us alone last night." She turned back to her picking. Everything was wet, but she didn't care. They may have been lucky last night, but they might not fare so well next time. She decided to pick all the peas that were even close to ready, instead of leaving some to ripen for a few more days.

When Phyllis came back, she said, "The deer wasn't here last night, Gram, but we know they'll be back. I need to have another shootin lesson."

"You need to practice. You have to set you up a target some place where you won't hurt nobody when you take a bad shot."

"I don't know where, Gram. Will you do it for me?"

"You can do it. You just don't want to be pointin at Andy's trail. That's all." She didn't say anything about Andy himself, and Phyllis didn't notice.

"But what should I shoot at?"

"Ask your dad for a bale of last year's hay."

"I should shoot the hay?"

"You can make a target on a piece of cardboard and put it on the bale. Then you can see how you're doin. That way you can correct your mistakes."

"I can do that. Where's Pop at?"

"He's down by the barn. He's gettin ready to mow as soon as things dry out enough."

"But where should I put my target, Gram?"

"Up the back field some place against the hill. Just fix it so you ain't pointin at Andy's trail."

"He don't go up there much these days. Most of the time, he hitchhikes to town. You can tell because he puts his good clothes on after supper."

"You still don't want to aim towards that trail. You never know who could be up there walkin around. You don't want to shoot nobody." She was pretty sure Andy had a camp up there where he could meet the hippie girl, but she didn't want to say that to Phyllis.

Phyllis went off with Moxie, and Nellie went on with her picking, but now she was in a hurry. She could hear the tractor running. When the hay was down, she would be busy for several days. She would like to get the chicken house cleaned before that, if possible.

But first she had to finish the peas, clean up the breakfast dishes and lay out something for lunch. Then she could sit in the rocker on the porch and shell peas until Frank and Phyllis and Andy came in.

She left the peas half done at lunchtime, and after that was cleaned up, she had a couple of hours to work on the chicken house. She got the wheelbarrow into position in the doorway and started to shovel. It wasn't deep. It wouldn't take that long. She worked fast. It was very hot. Sweat dripped off her forehead and ran down into her eyes, making everything blurry. She wouldn't let herself slow down—the rocker and the peas were waiting.

Suddenly she was weak and dizzy. Her heart raced, and the room spun around. She felt icy cold and sweaty at the same time. She was going to be sick to her stomach any minute. She held onto the wall and eased herself down onto one of the nesting boxes, hoping she wasn't sitting on some eggs. She felt too sick to look. Maybe it would leave as quickly as it had come, and she could get back to work.

After a few minutes, she realized that she needed to get to the house. Holding onto the wall, she made her way slowly to the door.

She managed to move the wheelbarrow enough to get out and close the door. No one was around to see her stagger to the house, and for that she could be grateful. She needed a little time alone, and then she would be all right again.

In the mudroom, she kicked off her boots and went to the kitchen, where she got herself a glass of water. She carried it out to the porch and sat down, and after a while, she could manage a few sips. She checked her pulse. Her heart had calmed down.

The peas gave her an excuse to be sitting down in the middle of the day, because she realized that she was going to keep this heart attack, or whatever it was, to herself. She didn't want to go to the doctor and find out that she would have to be careful and change what she was doing, maybe give up her beloved chickens, or even worse, move into town to be near the hospital, or move in with Helen and sit around all day just to stay alive a little longer. No, the best thing would be to keep her business to herself. If something was wrong with her heart, one day she would just topple over, and that would be the best for everybody.

She forced herself to drink all the water and to begin shelling the peas. That's what she was doing when a car drove up and stopped in front of the house. She thought it was a milk customer, until Ginny Alvarez got out of the car and reached back inside for a large pot, which she carried up the steps at the customers' end of the porch.

The door was closed between the customers' porch and the section where the family sat. Nellie thought about getting up and going to the kitchen to meet her, but she didn't feel that steady on her feet, so she shouted that she was out on the porch.

In a minute Ginny was standing in the doorway. "Here you are, Nellie. I brung you over a pot of beef stew to say thank you for the other day. Al's leg is healin up nicely. I put the stew on the back of your cookstove."

"You didn't need to go to that trouble, Ginny. That's what neighbors are for. You'd do the same for us."

"It ain't much, but at least you won't have to cook tonight."

"Perfect timin," Nellie thought to herself. Out loud she said, "Sit down and have a visit. We didn't have time for small talk the other day."

"Just for a minute. I can't stay. There's ten things I need to be doin at home right now. Are you goin in to see the fireworks tonight?"

"We can see 'em quite good from the porch here. That's what we usually do."

Ginny said, "I guess we'll make the trip if we get done in time. We didn't go in last night because of the rain." Then she disappeared. Nellie was beginning to wonder where she went, when she reappeared with a bowl from the kitchen. She scooped up some of the unshelled peas. "If I'm goin to sit, I can do a few peas. I couldn't stand to sit and do nothin while you was workin."

"I appreciate it."

"I see Frank's mowin up back."

"This is the last of it, unless he wants to try for a second cut. But Andy's goin to be leavin along in there sometime, so I don't know."

"Does Andy want to go?"

"I can't tell. He asks some questions about it. Frank wants him to."

"One of them Maxim boys went off to Canada. I don't know *what* to think about that. I have to say, girls are a lot of trouble, but there are advantages. At least they don't get drafted."

"Are your girls doin okay?"

"So-so. Millie's workin in town. She's got her own place in there. She likes it. Annie's thinkin of gettin married. I like him okay, but I hope they don't want to have a weddin." She poured the shelled peas into Nellie's bowl. "I gotta go. Stop down sometime when you're goin by."

"I'll do that, Ginny, and thanks. We'll get your pot back to you in a day or two."

Ginny left, and Nellie went on with the peas. So far, so good. Ginny certainly hadn't noticed anything.

CHAPTER 15

After supper, Cynthia helped Laura clean up. The whole time she was singing, "Come on, people now, everybody get together, try to love one another right now," in her head. It reminded her of Bob. They had had a short phone call from him, saying he was already in western Ohio. He had had some really far-out rides so far. He was going to start keeping a journal so he wouldn't forget any of his adventures on the road.

When they were done with the dishes, Cynthia went up to her room to change clothes. She almost wore a long skirt. She wanted to look beautiful for Andy, especially if this was the night when they finally got together, as the song said. At the last minute, she decided to wear blue jeans and sneakers, but she made up for the plainness by wearing her Mexican blouse with all the embroidered flowers on it.

She had to say something to Laura, so she went looking for her. She found her upstairs, getting Orion into his pajamas. She stopped in the doorway.

"Hi, Laura, I'm going for a walk in the woods."

Orion was lying on the big bed, while Laura changed him. She looked around at Cynthia. "The woods? It's almost dark. You can't."

"Well, I'm going to."

"But, Cynthy, you could get lost. It doesn't even make sense."

"It doesn't have to make sense. I'm going because I want to. Okay?"

Laura looked at her for a long, silent moment, and then she said, "You're meeting somebody up there, aren't you?"

"So what if I am?"

"Who...you don't know anybody...oh Lord, it's that boy at the Keyes farm, isn't it?" She finished dressing Orion and picked him up and gave him a kiss. Then she sat down in the rocker to nurse him. "That's who you're meeting, isn't it? I wish you wouldn't do that."

"Well, I'm going to."

"But you can't be serious. I mean, he's not like us."

"So?"

"He's so country."

"I don't care. I even like it that he's different."

"Do you like it that he comes from a family of hawks?"

"You don't *know* that."

"They've got a big American flag up. We all know what that means."

"I don't care. I'm only telling you where I'm going because I don't want you to see my car out front and look for me and get all worried when you can't find me. Just don't worry about me, okay? We can talk in the morning."

"Don't worry? Are you *crazy*? I'm already worried, and you haven't even left yet." She spoke louder than she meant to, and Orion's eyes popped open. He stared at his mother's face for a minute, and then he began to wail. Laura rocked him, murmuring to him to soothe him.

Cynthia saw her chance. "I'm going now. Let's talk in the morning. You'll see. It'll be fine."

She thought Laura nodded without looking up, and she didn't wait to find out.

She picked daisies as she walked up the hill through the tall grass. Long shadows lay across the field. The light was golden. She didn't want to take the time to make a crown of the daisies, but she tucked a few behind each ear as she walked. The top half of her looked like a flower child anyway.

Andy was standing under the apple tree, waiting for her. He must have been watching her walk up the field. When she got close to him, she said, "Hi Andy. Are we going to the camp? I'm glad you're here to show me the way." There was a lot implied by those words, and she felt uncomfortable.

But he took her hand and said, "Let's go," and the awkward moment passed as they went along the trail hand in hand.

"I had to tell my sister I was going to meet you."

"She probably didn't like it."

It was darker under the trees. The light was soft and dusky.

"I had to tell her something. I knew she would see my car out front and wonder where I was. But you're right. She tried to talk me out of meeting you."

He squeezed her hand. "I'm glad you didn't listen." There was an electric energy driving them both forward. "I told my family I was goin to hitch into town. I do that a lot, so they didn't notice. When I got partway down the road, I doubled back through the woods."

He had made some improvements to their camp since she was last there. The bed of pine boughs was covered with part of the tarp and a blanket, and some wood was laid ready beside the fire pit.

Andy dropped her hand. She was expecting him to put his arms around her and kiss her, but instead, he crouched down.

"What are you doing?" She was out of breath and disappointed.

"I'm makin us a fire."

"We don't need a fire. It's warm out, and you even brought a blanket."

"It'll cool off later, and anyway, the fire'll help keep the mosquitoes away."

"Mosquitoes?"

"They ain't found us yet, but they will."

She wished she hadn't noticed that he said *ain't*. It cooled things down a little. Laura would say, "I told you so."

She crouched beside him and kissed his shoulder. "I can help."

"It's okay. I got it."

All she could do then was watch while he nursed the tiny flames and fed them larger twigs as they grew. She tried to pay attention to what he was doing. She wanted to learn, but she was distracted by how close he was.

After a few minutes, he sat back. "Okay. That'll go."

She reached for him, and they stood up together, kissing. He tasted like smoke. She unbuttoned his shirt and pulled it open. There was a t-shirt under it. She pulled that up. His body was white in the firelight. She moved her hands over the muscles of his chest. His skin was smooth and cool. She slid her hands around his sides onto his back and pulled him close to her. He shivered.

Then she wanted her skin next to his, and she struggled with the

Mexican blouse. She hadn't thought when she put it on that it was tight under the arms and hard to take off. It took both of them to get her out of it. After that they pulled on each other's clothes and their own, until they both fell on the pine-bough bed, naked and laughing. They were all mixed up together and touching everywhere, skin to skin. The sweetness of it made her feel weak.

Then Andy sat up and started digging through the pile of clothes.

"What are you doing?" she said. "Are you leaving?"

"No, never. But I have to find somethin."

"What?"

"Somethin we need."

"Whatever it is, just leave it and come back."

"No, don't say that. I wouldn't do that. I got to find the condoms. They're in my pants pocket."

So then she helped him look for his pants. She would have skipped that step, but she was glad he was more sensible. She wished she could tell Laura, but she knew she couldn't.

They found his pants by the light of the fire, and after a few minutes he came back to her. The light was gleaming on his skin as he lay down beside her and began to kiss her again.

The pine branches creaked and snapped as they moved. They poked her in the back, but she didn't care. If there were mosquitoes around them, she didn't notice.

Afterwards, they lay still and spent beside each other. Everything smelled of pine and wood smoke. She lay at peace, looking up at the trunks of the trees above them in the firelight and beyond that, at the canopy of leaves with just enough space between them so she could see one bright point of starlight.

"Is that thunder in the distance?"

"It's the fireworks. They couldn't have 'em last night because of the rain."

"Where are they?"

"In the park downstreet. If we were on the other side of the hill, we could see 'em."

"I don't care. I can see a star through the leaves. That's enough."

After a while, Andy raised up on his elbow and looked at her lying naked in the light from the fire. He ran his hand along her side and down her thigh. "The first time I saw you, I thought you were the most beautiful girl I'd ever seen, but now that I see you without clothes, I see you are more beautiful than I even knew. I love you." He lay back down and sighed and closed his eyes. She waited, but he didn't say any more. The air was getting cooler, and the mosquitoes began to whine.

At first, she thought Andy must be asleep, but then he opened his eyes and said, "I'd better do somethin about them mosquitoes." He got to his feet and put some wood on the fire. It blazed up. He squatted before it like the first man in the world with the fire shining red and gold on his skin. The light made the surrounding forest even darker. They were enclosed in a bright circle like a small round room.

He looked around at her. "Even the smoke won't keep 'em away now they've found all this naked skin. We need to get under the blanket."

"I hate to stop looking at you," Cynthia said.

But he found the blanket and snapped it out so that it fell open over her. Then he climbed in beside her and put his arms around her, and a few minutes later he was asleep.

For a while she lay looking at him and thinking how wrong Laura was, how this whole night had been wonderful, unlike anything she had experienced before, not that she had had much experience either, but the few encounters she'd had were awkward fumbles compared to this.

The next thing she knew, the light was gray with dawn. Andy wasn't under the covers. He was standing by the fire, and he was dressed.

"Don't get up," she said. "Come back."

"I need to go down to milk. I didn't know whether to wake you or not. Can you find your way down without me?"

"I think so. Come back under the covers until you have to go." She raised the blanket so he could climb in.

He started to take off his shirt, and then he said, "No. I can't." He buttoned his shirt again. "If I get under there, I won't come out. And if my dad goes to the barn and sees that Rosie ain't been milked…well, I can't chance it. Throw some dirt and ashes on the fire to smother it before you leave, will you?"

When she woke up again, it must have been much later. The light was strong. She got dressed and folded the blanket and covered the coals of the fire with handfuls of dirt. She did it all slowly, looking down the trail to see if Andy might be coming back, but finally, she decided that she needed to get going. She had no idea how late it was, but if Laura was up, she was probably worried. And anyway, there was no food at their camp, and she was hungry.

CHAPTER 16

Andy hurried up the trail and down the other side. He didn't know what time it was, but he knew the only way to get himself to leave Crystal was to think he had to hurry.

The light was still pale with dawn, and the shadows lay long across the back field. He could smell the fresh-cut hay. Partway down, he stopped and picked up a handful. It was green and wet with dew, but it smelled just right. It would make good hay if the weather held.

The kitchen was dark and quiet. The big clock said five forty-five. He tiptoed up to his room and lay down on his bed to wait until it was time to milk.

Last night seemed like a dream or a scene from a movie. It was hard to believe it had happened to him. All he could be sure of was that he was determined to have more times like that. His attention was focused on what he could do to make it happen again, rather than on what had already happened.

Later, when he brought the bucket of milk into the kitchen, everyone was at the table having breakfast. Even Phyllis was there.

Pop was talking about the hay. "Here you are, Andy. I was just sayin we ought to be able to get that hay in tomorrow, but we'll have to ted this mornin and again this afternoon. I'm countin on you for that."

"Okay, Pop." Gram put a plate of bacon and eggs down in front of him. He was glad when Phyllis started talking so he could eat.

"Can I have a bale, Pop? Gram said I should ask you. I need it to shoot at."

Ma groaned when she heard, but nobody paid attention.

"You mean one of the *new* ones?"

Phyllis squirmed in her chair. "We could leave one at the top of the field when we pick up tomorrow. Then I wouldn't have to carry it all the way up."

"You ain't goin to take new hay to *shoot at*, Phyllis. Use your head! Get a no-good old one. It'll do just as good for a target."

"But Pop…"

Pop didn't say anything, but Andy could see he was fuming, so he said, "Get a old one and put it in the truck tomorrow, Phyllis. Okay? We have to go right up there." He picked up his dishes and took them to the sink and went out to strain the milk.

After a few minutes, Phyllis was there. "Thanks, Andy. I'll do like you said."

When he finished the milk, he went to find Pop. They hitched up the tedder, and Andy greased everything, waiting until the hay was dry enough.

It didn't take long to drive the back field and the little one they called the east corner. The whole time he was wondering if Crystal was at the camp. When he got both fields tedded, Andy left the tractor at the top near his trail. If anyone saw it there, they would think he just stepped off to take a leak in the woods. He trotted up the trail and down the other side to the camp. The fire was carefully put out. Everything was neat, but Crystal wasn't there. He thought about leaving her a note, but he didn't have any paper, and there was only charcoal to write with.

Around two o'clock he went up to ted again. He was on one of the last rounds of the back field when he happened to look up at the tree line. Crystal was sitting there, watching him. His heart gave a lurch of delight. He smiled, but she was too far away to see his face, and he couldn't wave in case someone down by the house was watching.

When he finished the back, he drove into the east corner field and stopped out of sight of the house. He left the tractor running and went through the woods to where Crystal was sitting.

She saw him coming toward her and stood up. "I saw you driving the tractor."

"Do you want a ride?"

"Really?"

"I got that little field still to do. It's around the corner so they can't see us from the house. Pop don't want nobody to ride. He says it's dangerous."

"If he doesn't want…"

He put his hand on her back as they walked. He wanted to take her in his arms, but she was so clean, and he was covered with dust and sweat.

When they got to the tractor, he boosted her up and had her sit on the seat, while he stood in front of her to drive. He put the tedder down, and they started around the field. She moved her hands from the tractor seat to his waist. He couldn't see her face, but he could feel how excited she was.

The roar of the engine, and the bang and clatter of the tedder made it impossible to say anything. They were enclosed in a world of heat and dust and noise, but they were in it together, and that made it the place he wanted to be.

When the field was done, he stopped the tractor out of sight of the house below. He helped her down and walked to the trail with her.

"That was far out. I've never done anything like that before," she said. She stepped close to him and kissed him on the lips.

He kissed her back and then pulled away so he could see her face. "Go up to the camp. I'll be there as soon as I take the tractor down. Wait for me. Okay?"

"I'll always wait for you, Andy."

He watched her walk away up the trail. What she said was just what he wanted to hear, but almost more than he dared to believe. Still, whatever happened next, he had already been luckier than he would have thought possible.

He took the tractor down and parked it in the barnyard. In the house he washed his hands and face and got a drink of water. No one was around. He ran up to his room and grabbed his alarm clock. It was just three-thirty. He had time to be with Crystal before he had to milk, and he didn't want to waste any of it, the way he had this morning.

When he got to the camp, she jumped up and came to him. He set the clock down on a rock and put his arms around her.

"What's that?" she said.

"A clock, so I know when I have to leave. I went earlier than I needed to this mornin."

"I know," she said, pressing herself close to him. "I was so sad when you left." Then she picked up the clock and looked at it. "Mickey Mouse?" she said laughing.

And that was the first he remembered how childish his clock was. "That's Phyllis's clock," he said. "I took it from her room."

"But she's going to need it."

"She won't. She's got another one."

"Is the other one a Minnie?" She was still laughing. Did she know he wasn't telling the truth? He could feel the red creeping up his face, making it worse.

He sat down on the pine-bough bed. She sat down beside him. "Do you have to do more work on the hay?"

He was glad to talk about something besides his stupid clock. "Not until tomorrow. If it's dry enough, we'll pick it up and put it in the barn."

"I want to help. I remember how fun it was last time."

She was sitting so close to him. His need was immediate and strong. He put his arms around her, but she pulled away. He said, "Am I too dirty for you?"

"Oh no. I love the way you smell, like sweat and machinery. It's very cool."

"What then?"

"Suppose somebody comes along and sees us?"

He laughed. "Who's goin to walk in your sister's woods when it ain't even huntin season? Come on. We don't have much time."

"I know you're right. It's my middle-class fear. I'm trying to shut out that voice in my head that wonders what people would think if they saw us together."

That hurt, but he pushed it aside. "I don't care what people think."

"I know. That's one of the things I love about you."

"So what're you waitin for?" He took off her shirt. It came off much more easily than the one last night.

He kissed her bare neck. Underneath the shirt was a bra. He hadn't remembered that from last night. "How do I get this thing off?"

She laughed and reached up her back to unfasten it. Then he was kissing her breasts and smooth stomach and after that he was so close that he really had to hurry. He couldn't take the time to make sure it was good for her.

When they were both lying spent with their clothes partly off, he said, "Was it okay for you?"

"Oh yes," she said. "I forgot all about other people."

"Me too."

After a few minutes, she raised up on her elbow and looked at him. "I want to get so I don't ever care what other people think or say. I know what *I* think, and that's all that matters." She lay back down beside him. "I don't care what anybody thinks...except for you, of course."

He was just drifting, half asleep, although a small part of him thought he ought to look at the clock, but right then he didn't care about anything.

Then she said, "But there is one place where you're not thinking for yourself. I just realized it."

"What's that?" He was stroking the smooth skin of her side. He wasn't really asking. He wasn't really thinking about anything.

"You say you don't care what other people think." She raised up, looking at him again. "But you're willing to let them tell you to go into the army, even when you know they're going to send you around the world to kill people. That's not thinking for yourself."

Suddenly, Andy was wide awake. He managed not to say anything, but he thought, "Oh no, not this again." All he wanted was the summer, and then he would deal with the army and the war. He even knew Crystal was right. He wasn't thinking for himself. He accepted what Pop and everybody he knew thought about Vietnam.

"But what about you?" he said. "Doesn't everybody do that?"

"Do what? What do you think I do?"

"Not just you. Everybody listens to the people they know. Don't you do that too?"

"I don't know what you're talking about. This war is wrong, and everybody that pays any attention knows it is."

Her voice had a hardness he hadn't heard before. It was okay for her to correct his thinking, but evidently not okay for him to correct hers. Well, what did he know? He was a dummy. He had never been anywhere. She had gone to college. She was different, and she knew more than he did.

Andy looked at the clock. It was five-twenty. He was glad it was time to go milk. He got up and put on his clothes without saying anything. It was a tricky place, and he didn't know how to make it better. He decided he would have to think about it while he milked.

"I have to go," he said. He wanted to touch her, but she seemed too far away. "I'll be back around seven. Will you be here?"

"I'll try to be," she said meekly. So that was the way they left it.

He got back to the camp a little after seven, but she wasn't there. He made a fire and sat beside it, thinking about what could have gone wrong. She was right about him believing what Pop and all the guys in his class said about serving your country when you are asked to. He needed to examine his beliefs before he left, and it looked like he would have some time to do that. It wasn't how he wanted to spend the next six weeks or whatever it was he had left, but it was probably the way it was going to be. Anyway, he had learned something, even if it was too late to do any good. She might question his beliefs, but he couldn't question hers.

He left the camp around nine-thirty. It had been full dark for a while, so he knew she wasn't coming.

He didn't know what to do about the clock. There wasn't much sense in leaving it at the camp, and he would need it in the morning down at the house. He could always bring it back if he was lucky enough to see her again. Some of his friends got wristwatches as presents when they graduated, but his family couldn't afford such expensive gifts.

The next day the weather was still good, and the hay was ready. In the early afternoon, Gram was up in the back field raking, and Pop was starting to bale.

Andy and Phyllis drove up to the top of the field with the bale

Phyllis had put in the truck. She climbed in back and threw it out and then jumped down and came over to the window. "I'm just goin to set it back in the woods, Andy, so we won't pick it up by mistake."

"Okay," he said. He drove along the outside windrow where Pop had already made bales. Right away, they got into their regular routine where Andy drove and threw in bales, and Phyllis stacked them.

They had picked up a couple of rows when Crystal came out of the woods. Andy caught the look of surprise on Phyllis's face when she saw her. He just hoped Gram and Pop were too busy to notice, but they were certain to wonder later how she got to the back field without a car.

Crystal was struggling to drag a bale to the truck when he ran to help her. "Where were you last night?" he said as low as he could. He took the strings of the bale.

She smiled at him. "I can do it. I need to build up my muscles."

"Okay, but I still want to know where you were."

"Did you go to the camp?"

"I was there until it got dark. That's when I figured you weren't comin."

Her smile was teasing. "Maybe I got there after you left."

He couldn't say anything in reply because they were so close that Phyllis could hear.

When they got to the truck, Crystal said, "Hi, Phyllis. I'm here to help. Just tell me if I don't do it right."

Andy threw in the bale and went to get another. When he got back to the truck, Crystal was leaning on it, talking to Phyllis.

"Come on," he said. "We've got work to do. I'm goin to pull ahead."

Crystal jumped up on the tailgate and sat with her legs dangling over. Andy wanted to tell her not to sit like that, but he couldn't say anything with Phyllis right there, so instead, he drove ahead very cautiously, worrying about hurting her beautiful legs on the uneven ground where the truck could bottom out.

When they had enough of a load, Andy drove down to the barn. Crystal sat very close to him. She didn't seem angry anymore, but neither of them could say anything with Phyllis there.

At the barn he stopped. Phyllis said, "We have to get out, Crystal. You don't want to ride up the ramp. It's too scary."

When she was getting out, she bumped into Andy quite hard. She said, "Excuse me!" and smiled at him in a way that made his heart lurch.

Crystal and Phyllis stood together watching while he backed up the ramp. When the truck was in the barn, they went in too.

"You have so much more hay than the last time I was here. I didn't realize. I wish I had known. I could have helped."

"We're all done now, unless we do a second cut. But Pop thinks we have enough, don't he, Andy?"

"Pop always wants to try for a second cut if the weather cooperates."

Phyllis climbed up on the load and threw a bale down near them. "Come on, guys. We got work to do."

After that they worked in silence. Phyllis slammed bales down flat on the floor, raising clouds of dust. Andy and Crystal passed each other taking the bales to the stacks. When the truck was empty, they went back up the hill for more.

Andy had no idea what was going to happen when all the hay was in the barn, but there was nothing he could do about it. He would just have to wait and see.

Gram raked the east corner field and then drove down to the house. Pop went into the little field and baled it, while they waited by the truck. Then Pop took the baler down to the house.

When they started to pick up the few bales, not even enough for a load, Crystal walked off into the woods. Phyllis must have seen the look on Andy's face, because she said, "Crystal told me to say goodbye to you. She said she'd be over to see us soon. She wanted to go back to her walk in the woods."

They had all the bales. Phyllis jumped out of the back of the truck. "She's nice, isn't she, Andy? I like her a lot. I think you should get her for a girlfriend."

"You mean, Crystal?" he said stupidly.

Phyllis went around to get in the passenger seat. Andy was glad she wasn't looking at him. He was afraid his face would start getting red.

"I can tell she likes you. She probably wants to be your girlfriend."

"I don't think so. Do you want to drive?"

"You can do it. You were too busy loadin the hay to notice her. I saw how she looked at you."

Andy got in, and they started driving down to the barn. "Well, it don't matter. I'm goin to be in the army soon. She wouldn't want a boyfriend who was goin to get killed."

"You shouldn't say stuff like that, Andy. You don't know what's goin to happen."

"You don't either, Phyllis. Anything can happen, and we got to get unloaded so I can milk."

CHAPTER 17

It was not even close to dark when Cynthia got to their camp. After the first few days, they had developed a routine of meeting in the evening and spending the night together. Andy always got to the camp first, but tonight he wasn't there. Cynthia decided she would try to make a fire by herself. That would make her feel more at home. She didn't want to think about what she would do if he didn't show up.

She was standing by the fire pit, thinking how to begin, when she heard a twig breaking in the woods behind her. She whirled around. It was Andy coming through the trees. She hoped he didn't see the look of fear that passed across her face before she saw who it was.

He was smiling. They met at the edge of the clearing and put their arms around each other. Cynthia spoke first. "I was just about to see if I could make a fire."

"Let's do it together. There's a pile of kindlin and stuff I got ready last night."

They crouched side by side, building a little pile for the fire to climb on. They started out working together, but soon it was Andy making the fire while Cynthia watched, hoping to remember enough to be able to do it alone next time.

Andy said, "I was afraid you wouldn't be here tonight."

"I don't know why. I said I would be."

He was quiet for a minute, and then he said, "It's me, not you. I can't believe this is happenin."

"What's happening?"

"I guess I can't believe someone like you would choose someone like me."

"That sounds like an old song."

"I'm serious. I can't believe it's true." He said all this without looking at her.

"Well, it is true," she said. "Give me your matches. I want to light the fire. It's almost dark."

"We ought to have some candles."

"I can get some from Laura. She won't notice. She has so many."

The fire blazed up, and they sat back together on the pine-bough bed.

"Phyllis keeps saying I should ask you to be my girlfriend."

"What do you tell her?"

"I say I don't know if you want a boyfriend who...a boyfriend like me."

The firelight was shining on his face. He looked worried. She kissed him. "You've got plenty of proof that I do." Then she remembered. "I almost forgot," she said. "I brought you a present, something I think you will like."

"I have everythin I could ever want already."

"Wait. You'll see." She reached her hand under the pine boughs and pulled out the weed and paraphernalia that Bob gave her before he left. "Ta-da," she said, holding up the bag.

"What is it?"

"Marijuana. Bob gave me his stash when he left. He gave me all his smoking equipment too. He couldn't take it because he was going to hitchhike."

Andy looked dismayed.

"Want to try it?" she said. "Don't look so worried. Have you ever smoked weed?"

"No, and I don't want to."

They had been sitting close together, but now he shifted a little away from her.

"Just try it. You'll see."

"No, I don't want to. It could turn me into a criminal."

"You'll like it, Andy. It makes everything more fun."

"I don't want to like it. I don't want to go to jail."

"What are you talking about?" She started to laugh. Then she saw how serious he was. "You don't really *believe* that, do you?"

"I saw it in a movie."

"Movies aren't true."

"This one was. They showed it to us in health class to warn us what could happen if you smoked that stuff."

"And you believed it?" She looked at him sitting beside her in the firelight. In some ways he knew so much, things she wanted to learn, like how to build a fire or milk a cow. In other ways, he was so gullible. "They want you to do what they say—they want you to go to the other side of the world to kill people. They can't stand it when you ask them *why* you should do such a thing."

"You've said that lots of times before."

She kissed his lips where the firelight shone on them. "Okay. I won't say any more. I'm just telling you what I know. I don't want you to do what I say. I want to be with you. That's all."

"That's what I want too."

They were sitting close together again, minutes from tumbling backward in each other's arms. They seemed to have gotten past the bad place.

But Cynthia couldn't resist trying to convince him. "I've only smoked a few times, and every time it has made everything better. It's like the world slows down and speeds up at the same time, and everything gets really intense. It's a wonderful feeling."

Andy didn't say anything, but she could tell he was listening.

"Everybody says it makes sex even better."

"Okay, okay. Don't say any more," he said, staring into the fire. "I could try it once, I guess. The guy in the movie was doin it all the time. That's when he turned crazy. *You* did it a few times, and you're still all right. I guess I could try it once."

"I'll roll us one," she said quickly. She didn't add, "before you change your mind," but that's what she was thinking. She got out a paper and some weed and started to roll it up. She'd never done the actual rolling before. She had only watched while other people did it. There wasn't much light. She was slow and clumsy, but finally she made a passable joint. "There," she said, holding it up so they could both see it.

The matches were still lying by the fire. She lit the joint, took a deep drag, and handed it to Andy. He took it with the tips of his fingers and sat there looking at it. She motioned for him to take a puff. She couldn't speak because she was still holding the smoke in her lungs.

She wanted him to see how to do it right.

He put the joint up to his lips and took a tiny sip of smoke, which he spat out immediately. He looked so prissy and disapproving that she burst out laughing, and all the smoke came out at once. "You look like an old lady. That's not the way you do it."

"I took a puff of smoke. That's what you did."

"You have to take it down into your lungs and hold it there. You spat it right out. Give it here. I'll show you." She took a deep drag. She could feel the slight dizziness that meant it was beginning to kick in. She held the joint out to him. "You try," she said, letting the smoke escape. "Keep it in for a while."

"Yeah, I remember now. That's what they told the guy in the movie. That's how he got hooked."

She took another puff. She could see that he was talking himself out of it. He wasn't even going to try. She was beginning not to care.

But then he said, "Okay," and reached out his hand. "I'll do it like you said." He took a gulp of smoke and tried to hold it in, but he started to cough, and it all came out.

"Wow." He took another mouthful. This time he held it longer before he began to cough.

Cynthia was too surprised to say anything.

When the coughing fit was over, he smiled at her and said, "Am I doin it like I'm supposed to?"

"Now you are. Do you like it?"

"I don't know." He thought for a minute. "I don't feel any different." He thought again. "Wait. Maybe everythin seems fine. Nothin to worry about. That's different, ain't it?" He lay back on the pine boughs, laughing.

Cynthia lay back beside him. They kissed and took drags and kissed some more. He was doing it her way, but he liked it. The kissing and the smoking didn't seem to be leading anywhere, but that was all right.

After some time had passed, Cynthia began to feel hungry. She said, "I'm starving. What about you?"

"I was just thinkin we ought to have some food up here. Can you cook?"

"Not much. Can you?"

"A little. On a campfire." He sat up. "But we have to go find somethin before we can cook it." He stood up. "You could stay here, and I could bring some food back."

"No. Wait a minute. I want to come with you." The idea of staying alone in the middle of the dark forest sobered her. "Where are we going?"

"I don't know. I have to think. You sure you want to come with me?"

"Definitely. What's the use of staying here by myself?" That was a way of saying it, without mentioning that she was afraid. "Where shall we go?"

"It depends on what time it is." They looked at the Mickey Mouse clock. It was eleven twenty-five. "No one wouldn't be up at my house, not after eleven."

"Laura and Paul might be, especially if Orion was fussy."

"That settles it. We'll have to try my house. We'll have to try the refrigerator."

"I don't care what it is. I just want some food."

Andy stirred the fire and put ashes over the pieces of wood that were still burning. "There. If we find somethin to cook, we can build it up again."

Andy went first, and Cynthia followed so close behind him that every once in a while she stepped on his heels. That made them both giggle. They went up to the top of the hill and down on the Keyeses' side.

Cynthia's back felt crawly. Some wild creature might be right behind her, but she didn't dare look around to see.

When they got to the field, there was more light. They walked toward the dark house. She could see Andy walking beside her in the starlight, but if they could see each other, anyone awake in the house could see them. When they got about halfway down the field, a dog began to bark.

"That's Phyllis's new dog, Moxie. Phyllis must of put her on the back porch, so she could bark if any deer got in the garden." He was whispering. "I just hope Pop don't hear her and flip on the floodlight. We're sittin ducks right now."

They hurried the rest of the way down to the house with Andy speaking softly to the dog to keep her from barking. She was on a long rope. She came partway up to meet them.

"Phyllis must of fixed her rope so she could go around the corner of the house to see the road in front. If you go over there out of sight and hold onto her, I'll see what I can get for us."

Cynthia crouched around the corner, holding Moxie by her collar and whispering to her. She hoped Andy would hurry. Moxie smelled awful. She probably couldn't smell anything but herself.

After a while Cynthia heard Andy's steps on the porch. "Did you get us some food?"

"Yeah. I want to give Moxie a bite, and then we can go." He broke off a piece of something, which Moxie downed in one gulp.

They hurried up the field along the tree line, hoping no one would see them. When they got to the top of the field, Cynthia was out of breath. "Stop a minute," she said. "I'm dying of hunger. What'd you get us? Let's have some right now."

"Hot dogs. We can cook them over the fire."

"I want something right now. I don't think I've ever been this hungry."

Andy stopped walking. "I got a loaf of bread too. Gram will know, but she won't say nothin." He opened the bag and handed her a slice.

"Store-bought Wonder Bread," she said, thoughtfully. "When you said bread, I pictured something wonderful and homemade."

"It's still food, and you don't have to eat it if you don't want to."

"Oh, I'll eat it. I just thought your Gram would make her own bread."

"She does once in a while."

They ate slices of the fluffy, tasteless bread while they walked. When they got back to the camp, Andy stirred up the fire and put on some more wood. He took out his pocketknife and went a few steps into the trees to cut some sticks for skewers. He whittled a sharp point on one of the sticks, put a hot dog on it, and held it out to Cynthia, but she had pulled a stick out of their bed and was already holding a hot dog over the fire, proud of herself for being so efficient.

After a few minutes, her stick flamed up, and the hot dog dropped into the fire. "Damn," she said. "It was almost ready."

Andy poked at it, pulling it to the edge of the fire. He picked it up, brushed the ashes off and tried to hand it to her, but she wouldn't take it.

"No," she said. "It's too dirty."

Andy ate it himself and handed her his hot dog on its stick. "It's just ashes," he said. "It's really tasty. Here. Take mine. You've got to use green wood for the stick. You see what happens when the wood is dry."

Cynthia started to eat the hot dog right off the stick. It was so hot she burned her mouth, but she didn't care.

They cooked and ate the whole package and most of the fluffy bread. Then they both lay back on the creaking pine branches, full of food and laughing. Cynthia was going to try to roll them another joint, but before she could find where she put her stash, Andy was asleep and even snoring a little. She found the blanket and spread it over both of them and went to sleep beside him without even taking off her clothes.

CHAPTER 18

When Nellie was washing up the breakfast dishes, Andy came in. After he put the milk through the strainer, he stopped in the doorway.

"Can I dig a few potatoes out of your garden, Gram?"

Nellie shut off the water and turned around. "What for?" she said, although she knew. She was looking for a way to confront him about the food he took. No one else would have taken all the hot dogs and a loaf of bread during the night without Moxie even barking.

"I want to cook them at my camp up in the woods." He was looking down at the floor.

"Well," she said. "That's nice. Do you need some pots and pans for your camp?"

She watched him relax a little when he saw she wasn't going to ask him why he needed a camp so close to the house. "We don't...I mean, I don't have any pots. I was plannin to cook the potatoes in the ashes, but they get pretty dirty that way."

She hadn't ever noticed Andy minding a little dirt before. "I'll give you my old Dutch oven. You can cook a lot of different things in that. You can even bury it in the coals and use it like a oven if you want to."

A smile spread across his face.

"I'll give you a old kittle for boilin water too. You ought to be all set with them."

"Thanks, Gram. I won't keep 'em very long. The army's goin to have to feed me pretty soon."

"You're goin in then?"

"I guess so. I mean, I ain't got no choice."

"Ginny said one of them Maxim boys went over to Canada so he wouldn't have to go."

"I couldn't do that. I mean, how could I?"

"How did the Maxim boy do it?"

"I don't mean *that*. I guess I could get there pretty easy, but I couldn't never come back again. I would have to stay there forever."

"Yes," Nellie said. "That would be hard. It would be hard for all of us."

"I've lived here my whole life. I love this place the way you do, Gram. Think what it would feel like if you couldn't never come back again."

"Oh, Andy honey, I know. It's such a hard choice. When I think I wouldn't never see you again, my old heart just about breaks...and then I think, well, I wouldn't see him again if he got killed in Vietnam, so this sounds like a better idea to me. And I know I said you ought to talk to your dad about what you should do, and I know your dad always tells me to stay out of it, because I don't know nothin about it, and I know he's right that I don't, but I don't care what he says, I don't think you ought to go to war. We ain't got no business over there. It's somebody else's fight, and you could get killed for nothin."

"Do you really think I should go to Canada? What would Pop say if I ran away like that?"

Nellie sighed. "He's gonna have plenty to say, but, honey, is that gonna stop you?" She looked at him standing there with so much trouble in his young face. He hadn't even had a chance to grow into his looks yet, and someday he would be even better looking than he was now—if he lived, of course. She wanted to memorize everything about him, because *whatever* he did, the likelihood was that she wasn't ever going to see him again.

"But, Gram..."

"Honey, I believe your dad was a good soldier, and it was important for him to go to war. But them was different times. It was a different war. He knew what he was fightin for."

"He's goin to say I'm a draft dodger and a coward. That's what he always says about the protesters. He's goin to say he took his turn to fight for his country, and now it's my turn to do my duty."

"Yes, he will, but nobody shouldn't go to war unless they believe in what they're fightin for. And you don't, do you?"

He thought for a minute before he answered. "I guess not. I don't understand what Pop says about the commonists takin over our country. I mean, how would they even get here?"

"You ain't like your dad, you know. You got a lot of your ma in you—a gentleness, I guess you could call it. I remember how you was always findin some little creature that you had to take care of.

Remember them kittens that you nursed when their mother died? I can't imagine your dad would of taken all that trouble. Remember how you used to get up in the night to feed 'em?"

Andy smiled at that. "Some of them cats is still here."

"See, Andy, what's right for your dad ain't necessarily what's right for you. You got to do what's right for you."

He hugged her then. "Thank you, Gram. It helps me. I still don't know what I'm gonna do, but now I can sort it out better. You always help me."

She patted him on the back. "This is a hard place, Andy, but we'll get through it." She took a few steps back and knelt down by the cupboard with the pots in it. "Now let me find you them pots I said you could have."

She had to take out quite a few pots before she got to the back of the cupboard, but she was glad Andy couldn't see that she had tears in her eyes from thinking about him going to war. She dragged out the little cast iron Dutch oven she used to use when she first got married, and it was just the two of them.

"Here you go, Andy. You see how there's a lip all the way round the lid? That's so you can pile the coals on top when you want it for a oven, but you can use it like a fryin pan too. We used it like that all the time. Set it up on the counter. I got to put all this stuff back." When that was done, she handed him the kettle and stood up slowly. Her knees creaked.

Andy hovered around. "I could of done that for you, Gram."

"I'm too set in my ways, but thank you, honey."

Andy was just about to leave with his pots when she stopped him. "I got one more thing to say. Now you can cook your own food. You don't need to sneak in and take ours. I could of been in a spot if we didn't have some leftovers."

He opened his mouth, but no words came out. He looked so unhappy she was sorry she'd said anything. "Get yourself out some hamburg to go with the potatoes. Just remember to ask before you take stuff."

He nodded. "I promise, Gram."

She would have hugged him again, but his arms were full, so she just said, "Get goin. I got work to do."

After he left, she turned on the water and finished the dishes, but all the time she was thinking about how she was going to try to finish cleaning the chicken house. She hadn't told any of them what happened when she started the job, and that was weeks ago. If she was careful to pace herself, it wouldn't happen again. So far, the only aftereffect was that she got very emotional, but she had managed to keep the others from noticing.

If she *did* get weak and dizzy today, she would have to tell Frank, and that would cause trouble for everybody. After all, she was as old as the century. It wouldn't be surprising if things were starting to go wrong with her.

She shoveled out three wheelbarrow loads of manure and dirty hay. Frank wasn't around, so she took a bale of this year's hay to replace what was dirtied. She liked her chickens to have the best, and right now it was especially important, since she wanted to take some of them to the Tunbridge fair in September.

She thought about Andy too, and how he thought he might die soon in Vietnam. It made her feel like crying. She wanted to tell him that her situation was not the same as his. She was at the end of a long life when her body was beginning to fail. She wanted him to see how different that was from his case, young and just at the beginning of his journey. Everything was still ahead for him. He didn't need to go to war and ruin his future.

But what could she say? Young people didn't understand that life could be long, with many directions and fresh starts. They didn't know that because they hadn't experienced it yet.

The chicken house looked and smelled fresh when she finished. The chickens were delighted. They walked around, inspecting her work, clucking to each other and pecking at the new hay.

Nellie went into the house. She was pleased with herself. She felt just fine, hardly even tired. No one needed to know what had happened. She would be good for a while longer.

CHAPTER 19

Andy thought about going up the hill through the back field. Now that all the hay was in the barn, the mowed field made for easy walking. The Dutch oven was heavy, heavier because of the potatoes he got from the garden, and then there was the meat and the kettle. It was an awkward load.

Gram knew about his camp in the woods, but no one else did. Pop wouldn't like it, and if Phyllis knew, she would come snooping around. It was better to go through the woods on the game trail. It was slow, but it was private.

When he finally reached the camp, he left the kettle there and took the Dutch oven to the little pool in the brook where they got water. He put the frozen hamburger, wrapped in its paper, on the bank and the Dutch oven into the middle of the little pool. The water came just over the side of the pot. He swirled the potatoes around, rubbing them with his rough hands until they looked clean. Then he set them out to dry on the grassy bank.

Back at the camp, he laid out tinder and some sticks to start a fire. He kept looking for Crystal, hoping she would show up, but she still hadn't arrived when the Mickey Mouse clock said it was almost five and he had to go milk. She was probably waiting until later to meet him. She knew his schedule. He was *almost* sure she would come.

And he was right. When he got back to the camp, she was there, crouched over a tiny fire. She blew on it, but it flickered and threatened to go out. She tossed her long hair back over her shoulder and crouched lower to blow again. He watched, thinking how lucky he was to have such a beautiful girlfriend.

Then she looked around and saw him. She smiled. "You got here just in time. What am I doing wrong? The fire refuses to go."

Andy bent down and rearranged the sticks. The fire flared up.

She smiled at him. "It's magic! How did you do it?"

"Things just needed shiftin around." He put some larger sticks on top, trying not to feel proud of such a small accomplishment. "We want to build coals to cook on. I brought us some potatoes and hamburg. I hope you know how to cook it."

"I can try. I don't know much about cooking. Where is it? I brought some food too, but mine doesn't need to be cooked."

"It's down by the brook. I hope the meat is thawed by now. Gram gave it to us, and a pot to cook it in."

"Really?"

"And a kittle too. If we can just figure out how…. I'll go get it. You can put on some more wood."

In a minute he was back with the Dutch oven full of potatoes and the still-frozen meat.

"Wow," Crystal said. "That's a real dinner, not like mine. Here's what I brought us." A grocery bag was sitting on the blanket behind her. She pulled it over and took out three packages of cookies. "And look at this." She held up a big bag of marshmallows. "There are candles in here too. I poached some from Laura. She won't know. She has so many."

Andy stirred the fire, working on building enough coals to cook, and Crystal lit some of the candles and used the dripping wax to fasten them on the rocks around the fire pit. They both ate cookies steadily while they worked.

"I'm goin to put Gram's pot on the coals with the cut-up potatoes in it. We'll see what happens. I wish I had somethin to stir with." He broke off part of a stick. "This'll have to do. We could use some spoons, but Gram would be sure to notice if I took any." After pushing the potatoes around the pot, he said, "We need butter too, but that's easy. Gram makes butter almost every day."

Crystal was watching over his shoulder. When the potatoes began to clump together on the bottom of the pot, he dumped the ones he could get free onto the lid and put in the block of meat. It was soft on the outside, but still frozen in the middle. He stabbed off chunks of it with his pocket knife. The thawed chunks sizzled in the pan. Crystal kissed his shoulder. "I thought you didn't know how to cook."

"Let's see how it tastes," he said, but he was pleased that she was impressed.

The meat stuck to the bottom of the pan too. When it was all at least partly cooked, he poured the potatoes back in and mixed everything together.

After a few minutes, he took the pot off the fire, speared a bit of the mixture on the end of the stick and held it out to her.

She pushed it away. "You try it first. I'm not very hungry. I ate too many cookies, and I want some room for marshmallows."

Andy pretended to be Gram. "You need to eat some dinner first."

"No, I don't. This is our place. We can eat whatever we want."

That made him laugh. He sat down on the blanket beside her and ate a handful of the meat and potato mixture. "It's good. Don't you want to try it at least?"

"Maybe later. Not now."

He ate a few more bites. "Ah, nothin like a home-cooked meal." That made them both laugh.

Crystal lay back. Andy was just about to kiss her, when she pushed him away and started feeling under the blanket. "I put the weed under here so we could have some later. Want to?"

He felt a small twinge. They so often wanted different things. She hadn't even tried his dinner. "Right now I want some water." He stood up to go to the little pool. "Do you want me to leave the food for you?"

"No...I don't know. What should we do with all the leftovers?"

"I'm goin to put the lid on the pot and set it down in the brook. That can be our refrigerator. I don't think any critters can get to it because the lid is so heavy."

"Oh, that's cool! I love it."

That made him feel better. He put the Dutch oven in the shallows, with the water lapping the bottom of the pot. He was proud of himself for figuring out how to store their food.

When he got back to Crystal, she was lying on their bed, taking a puff of her joint. "Come have some. It's lovely."

He put a couple of sticks on the fire to give himself a moment to think about what he ought to do. The summer was half over, and he didn't want to waste it worrying about a future that might not exist. "All right," he said. He lay down beside her and took a long, dizzying drag.

For a while they took puffs in turn without talking. Then she said, "What do you want to do when you grow up?" It was as though she'd heard his thoughts about the future. But what did she mean about growing up? That sounded like she thought he was still a child.

He said, "I want to go on just like this for the rest of my life, however long that is."

"No, but I mean, *really*. What do you want to *do*? You can't stay in the woods forever."

"Who knows? Maybe I can." Making love was what he was thinking about right now.

"I'm serious. What are you planning to do for a job? Where do you want to live—all that?"

He sat up on one elbow to kiss her, but she turned her head, and the kiss landed on her cheek. "Tell me," she said.

"I don't know. I don't think about it much. I could just stay on the farm. There's plenty of work here." He was hoping he wouldn't have to get into the whole going-to-war thing.

"You'll have to make some money somehow. Is selling milk enough?"

"No, it ain't, but we sell other stuff too—calves sometimes, and wood if we get more than we need. Gram makes butter and sells eggs, and Ma works in an office downstreet. It adds up."

"Really?"

"And if it ain't enough, I can always get somethin in the feed store or the granite quarries."

For reply, she rolled into his arms and began to kiss him, apparently forgetting how soon he was going to be drafted. The idea of staying on the farm was only a fantasy that wouldn't come true for years, if ever, but that was something he was glad to forget also.

CHAPTER 20

On her way into Severance, Cynthia thought about how glad she was to help Laura, but she didn't feel that way toward the five people who were staying at the house right now.

They had been there for half a week already, two couples and a little girl, and they showed no signs of leaving any time soon. None of them helped with the cooking, or even with the dishes, and they managed to be stoned or somewhere else if buying groceries was even mentioned. They didn't seem to have any money, but they all had plenty of weed and sometimes other drugs, like LSD.

And then there was Flower, the little girl of one of the couples. Cynthia wasn't sure whose child she was. She didn't like *her* much either. She was always pestering Orion, trying to feed him, or trying to pick him up. Cynthia and Laura had to be constantly on watch because her parents, whoever they were, didn't seem to notice what she was doing.

Cynthia thought about it on her trip to the grocery store. They were out of everything. It was going to be a big load. Laura had asked her to go because she was too busy with all the extra cooking. If she was in Laura's place, she would have told them it was time to move on, but Laura was better at living up to the ideals of the counterculture than she was, and Cynthia had to respect that.

Later, when she came out of the store pushing her loaded cart, she passed a guy with long hair and a beard handing out an anti-war newspaper. When she brought the unloaded cart back to the store, she asked him for a couple of copies. He asked where she was living, and she told him about Laura's place and the people who were staying there. He had nice eyes, but too much tangled hair and beard.

On the way home she worried that Andy was making her less of a hippie. She wanted him to teach her how to go back to the land, but she didn't want him to mess with her political beliefs. And yet she had to admit that the whole summer, ever since she met him, she hadn't been spending much time thinking about the war. Even when Laura and Paul's friends were talking about protesting, she didn't join in. She was always busy figuring out how to get away, so she could spend time at the camp with Andy, and worse, if being with Andy was destroying her principles, she didn't care, because she was still going to try to get up in the woods to see him as soon as she could.

By the time she managed to get away, after helping Laura clean up the supper dishes, she was annoyed with everyone. It was almost dark, but luckily the moon was up and shining, so there was some light under the trees.

She hurried up the trail, feeling a little creepy, and afraid to look behind her, in case some creature was following her. She couldn't wait to get to Andy's arms and the light of the campfire.

She burst into the clearing, but Andy wasn't there. It was still and dark. She wasn't that late. Why wasn't he here? She put her hand onto the ashes in the firepit and pulled it back quickly. It was hot. He *had* been here. Why didn't he wait for her?

She felt like crying. It was getting darker by the minute. She managed to find the matches so she could light the candles that were stuck on the rocks, but that just made the outer darkness even darker, and she knew she would have to leave. It didn't feel safe and cozy without Andy.

She blew out the candles she had just lit, except for one. She pried that one off the rock and started walking toward the trail, trying to picture herself, a procession of one, under the cathedral arch of the trees, but she got more and more frightened. The little circle of light made everything else darker and scarier, until she blew out the candle and began to run, stumbling in her haste. She didn't slow down until she got to the field and the calming light from the moon.

The next day in the late afternoon she went up to the camp. Andy would be milking, but she wanted to get there early. She planned to leave well before dark if he didn't show up. She didn't want another scary trip alone through the forest.

She spent a long time making a fire, carefully blowing on the flames and feeding them tiny sticks. She was sitting back, admiring what she had built without help, when Andy said, "That's a good fire."

It made her jump. She hadn't known he was there. To cover her embarrassment, she said, "Where *were* you last night?"

"Here. Where were *you*? I stayed until dark. Then I figured you weren't comin."

"Well, I did. I got here as soon as I could get away from Laura and Paul and the others. The ashes were still warm, so I knew you'd been here. Why didn't you wait for me?"

He didn't try to defend himself. He just sat down beside her and put his arms around her. "Don't be mad. We're both here now. Let's not waste it."

The sweetness of the words diffused her anger. They fell back in each other's arms onto the bed of pine boughs.

Later, in the peaceful aftermath, Andy said, "Are you hungry?"

"Yes, I am. Have you seen that bag of marshmallows? It's around here some place. I'll look for it."

They sat by the fire, toasting marshmallows and talking. Cynthia said, "I was so disappointed that you weren't here last night. I went home to Laura's and took a long, hot shower. That's a luxury we don't have up here. It's lucky we both have places with running water so we can have baths when we need them."

She thought Andy would agree with her, but he didn't say anything. He was quiet for what seemed like a long time, staring into the fire and poking it with his stick. Finally, without looking at her he said, "There's somethin I've been wantin to show you. Maybe tonight's the right time."

"What're you talking about?"

"You'll see. It's a place. It ain't far." He started to cover the fire with ashes.

"If it isn't far, why are you messing up the fire?"

"We might could want to stay there for a while."

"Really? We might want to stay? Tell me where it is."

"Just follow me. You'll see. I can't tell it right in words."

"I don't see why you can't *try*."

But he wouldn't say any more. He just started walking, and she had to go with him or stay alone with the closed-down fire.

The moon was up. Its silver light shone through the black pillars of the trees. Andy was with her tonight, and the forest was different.

At the top of the hill, Andy turned and walked along the stone wall. Cynthia had only gone over the wall the way the trail went. She had never thought of following the wall into the woods.

The moon was behind them, shining on Andy's back. Ahead was the darkness of the nighttime forest. All she could do was stay close to him and wait to see where he was taking her.

She was looking at the way the moonlight touched his back, when he stopped so suddenly that she crashed into him. She peeked around his back, and what she saw made her say, "Oh my God. I don't believe it!"

There was a rectangular pool of water, just below the stones on Laura's side of the wall. A long shaft of moonlight lay the length of it, making a shining path of silver. Cynthia was transfixed by the beauty of it.

Andy sat down on the stone wall and started to take off his clothes.

"What're you doing?" she said.

"I'm goin in. Don't you want to try it? It's plenty deep enough to swim in." He stood on the bank, a column of white in the dark night. Then he did a shallow dive into the shaft of moonlight that lay the length of the pool. After a minute he appeared, shattering the perfect path of the light. He tossed his head. Drops of water flew in all directions. "Come on. What're you waitin for?"

Cynthia began to undress. She was slow. The air was chilly, and the water would be cold, but it was so beautiful that she wanted to be part of it.

She stepped into the shallow water on the edge. She felt shy to be standing outdoors with no clothes on, and the water around her ankles was icy.

She could have stayed where she was, trying to decide what to do next, but she lost her footing on the slippery bank and sat down hard in the water. When she stopped sliding, the water was up to her chest.

Andy was laughing at her. "That's one way to do it," he said.

She looked across the moon-spackled water to the dark trees on the other side. It was like a scene from a fairy tale, and she was in it. She couldn't spoil it by being annoyed by what he said.

She swam into the center of the moonlight, and Andy joined her there. They swam the length of the pool side by side, their white bodies disappearing into the darkness below. They swam in sync, like birds, flying and turning wordlessly together. At each end, as they turned, they exchanged a wet kiss.

For a long time, she wished it would go on forever, but then she began to feel tired and cold. "I'm going to get out, but let's come back. It's much better than a shower."

She climbed up the bank into the icy air and sat on the cold stone of the wall. She was wondering how she would dry herself, when Andy got out of the water. He put on his pants. Then he balled up his shirt and rubbed her back with it, warming and drying her.

"Your shirt's going to get all wet," she said, but she didn't want him to stop.

"It don't matter. We'll be back by the fire in a minute."

When they got back to the camp, Andy built up the fire, and they both dove under the covers with all their clothes on. They laughed and hugged as they warmed themselves and each other.

CHAPTER 21

The telephone rang just as Nellie finished cleaning up after breakfast. She thought it might be Helen, and it was.

At first Helen talked about how they were finally getting some sunny weather.

Nellie said, "It always settles down in August."

"Does it? I never noticed. Did you hear about the Sensi boy?"

"From West Severance? There's a huge Sensi family in West Severance."

"Yes, that's why I thought you would have heard."

"I didn't. Tell me."

"It's bad. He was a soldier in Vietnam."

"I can guess. He was killed."

"Yes, you're right. You're going to hear. They sent the body back to the family to be buried."

"I wonder if Andy knows."

"If he doesn't, he will soon enough."

"You don't know what happened, do you?"

"No, not yet, but he was a soldier in a war, so…"

"I wish Andy wasn't goin to have to go so soon."

"Well, Nellie, remember when Frank had to go fight. You worried so much, and he came home without even an injury."

"I know, but…"

After the phone call, Nellie got her sunhat and the wheelbarrow and went to the garden to pull the garlics. She always meant to dig the dirt away. She knew she shouldn't pull them out of the ground, but after she got the row started, they came out so easily that it was much quicker to pull them.

She worked her way along the patch, thinking about Andy and the war and the Sensi boy. She wondered if *he* wanted to be in it, if he chose to go. She got angrier and angrier, wrenching the garlics out of the ground. Maybe the Sensi boy didn't want to go. Maybe he only went because everyone said he ought to. And now he was dead. That could happen to Andy. She was beginning to think Andy would like to get out of it if he could.

CHAPTER 22

It was a sunny morning, hot and still, the best of early August. The funeral for Gary Sensi was at the Catholic Church in Severance. Andy had to hitchhike because Pop was too busy to go, and Gram said she didn't think her old heart could take it. It got complicated when Phyllis insisted on coming too. Ma probably wouldn't have let her go, but Ma was at work.

When they were standing at the bottom of the hill, Phyllis said, "Andy, wouldn't it be great if Crystal came along? She could go with us, and everyone would think she was your special girlfriend."

Andy had to pretend he thought it was a good idea, but he hoped it wouldn't happen. He wasn't sure what Crystal would say about the funeral of a Vietnam soldier. He hoped she wouldn't hear about it, even though everybody in town seemed to know.

Phyllis said, "Do you think Rickie will be there?"

"I don't know. He's still in boot camp, but maybe they'll give him leave because it's his brother."

That was when Vincent Johns from down the road stopped for them in his pickup. They both squeezed in, putting their feet on the tools and empty motor oil cans on the floor.

"Where're you kids headed?" he said when they were settled enough so he could get on the road again.

"We're goin to Gary Sensi's funeral."

Andy was quick to add, "You can leave us anywhere in town."

"I'll take you all the way. I'm goin to the funeral too."

"Wow!" Phyllis said. "That's cool. This is my first time hitchin. It's fun."

Vince and Andy looked at each other over Phyllis's head, but neither one of them said anything.

After a few minutes, Vince said, "There's goin to be quite a crowd. I don't know where I'll be able to park, but I can take you kids home after."

"That would be great," Andy said, before Phyllis had a chance to say anything different.

Vince had to park blocks away from the church. It looked like everyone was there. They thanked him and started walking, but before they got there, Phyllis saw some of her friends and went off to join them. Andy went into the church alone. It was dark and hushed, even though there were lots of people inside. He got in the line of people going by the coffin. Gary was two classes ahead of them in school, but Andy could remember seeing him in the halls. He was afraid of what he would look like in his coffin, but it was all right. He didn't look real, but he didn't look disfigured either. He even looked pretty much the way he had when he was alive.

Andy was wondering where he ought to go next, when he saw Rickie standing alone by the side wall. He went over to him.

"Hey, Andy, how's it goin?"

"I'm real sorry about your brother, Rickie."

"Yeah, I know. Mom's takin it hard."

Andy didn't know what to say about that. Finally, he said, "So, how's boot camp? They let you out to come home anyways."

"Yeah, they had to. It's called 'compassionate leave' or somethin. I've got to go right back after."

"That's too bad," Andy said. "I thought we could hang out together while you were here."

"Naw. They don't want me to have a good time. I'm supposed to go to the funeral and go right back."

Andy was secretly glad. Time with Rickie would be time away from Crystal, and he didn't dare introduce them to each other, because of what she might say about the war.

Andy couldn't think of anything else to say. He wished someone would come along to talk to them, when there was a loud cry from the front of the church. They both looked toward the coffin. A woman was standing there, flailing her arms at the people near her. She shouted, "Don't hold onto me. I need to see him."

Rickie said, "That's my mom."

Everyone watched as she walked unsteadily toward the coffin and leaned into it. She collapsed across the body with a scream.

Rickie said, "I gotta go."

Andy watched as Rickie and a lot of other people raised her up and half-carried her away. She was screaming hysterically.

Andy kept watching even after all the people had disappeared out the back in spite of her protests. When she was gone, people began to settle themselves into their seats, speaking to each other softly. There was a rustle of bodies and a hum of low voices.

Andy searched the crowd for Phyllis, but he didn't see her. He stayed where he was standing in the aisle, even after the priest came out to do the service, but he didn't hear much of what was being said. All he could think about was Rickie's mother. He looked around for her. Was she missing it?

Outside the church afterwards, Andy found Phyllis, but she wouldn't come with him. She wanted to ride to the cemetery with her friends. He left her there and rode with Vince. Rickie's mother wasn't at the burial, and Rickie wasn't there either.

In the truck going home, Phyllis couldn't stop talking about the commotion made by Rickie's mother. Andy tried to shut her up so that Vincent Johns wouldn't think she was some kind of monster, but he couldn't get her to be quiet. She babbled all the way to their house. When Vince left, she ran inside to find Gram so she could tell it all over again.

After he milked, he went up to their camp. Crystal was already there. "I've been waiting for you," she said. "I want to go for a swim. I ate a lot of cookies, so I'm not hungry. Let's go."

Andy was still numb, still thinking about the funeral, but he couldn't say anything. Crystal might answer with something he didn't want to know, like it was Gary's fault for signing up to be a soldier, or his mother's fault for letting him go. She didn't have any idea how things worked for people like them.

Andy went first up the trail. It was dusk, still light enough to see. It was going to be a dark night until the moon came up, but that would be much later. He knew he ought to figure out how they would get back to their camp in the dark, but he couldn't seem to focus his mind on it.

When they got to the pool, Crystal was surprised at how different it looked. It was because the moon wasn't up yet, but Andy didn't say anything. They both took off their clothes in silence, turned away from each other.

"Andy, are you mad at me?"

"No. Why?"

"Something's wrong. What is it?"

"I don't know. Nothin's wrong."

"Okay," she said. "Be that way." She walked to the edge of the water and stood there, a bright column in the almost-dark, but even that didn't bring Andy back. She did a short, shallow dive into the middle of the pool and came up shaking her head and laughing. Drops of water splashed in every direction. "What're you waiting for?" she said.

He couldn't answer that, so he dove in and came up near her. Everything seemed disconnected. Part of him was still back in the church with Rickie's mother fainting across the body of her soldier son. Nothing else seemed as real, not even Crystal's beautiful body. They swam across the pool side by side.

"What's going on with you, Andy?"

"Nothin."

"No, but something's wrong. I can tell."

He swam over to the edge of the pool and stood up.

"I did something that made you mad. What was it?" She stood up beside him. She was shivering.

"Nothin's wrong, except that you're cold." He went up the bank and got the towel she brought. "Get out and let me dry you." He could manage that, at least. But he wasn't really paying attention to her, just to the drops of water on her skin, and she noticed.

She snatched the towel and started to dry his chest, alternating drying and kissing the spot she had just dried. After a few minutes, she looked up into his face. "I don't know what's the matter, but something is. I'm going to get dressed."

"Me too." He wanted to apologize for being so out of it, but he didn't know how to say it.

They went back to their camp. It was a slow, stumbling walk because the moon wasn't up yet.

Andy built up the fire, and they got under the covers with their clothes on. For the first time ever, Andy was hoping they would just fall asleep without making love. He was horrified at himself and afraid she would notice. He pretended to go to sleep. Crystal snuggled up against him, and after a while, she fell asleep. He lay awake for a long time, wondering what could be wrong with him.

CHAPTER 23

Laura was standing at the stove cooking when Cynthia entered the kitchen. Orion was in his highchair, banging his spoon on the tray and laughing.

"That smells good, Laura. Where's Paul? His truck's not out front."

"He's up in back. There's a big limb down on the edge of the field."

"I saw that the other day."

"Paul's going to cut it up with his new chainsaw…if he can."

"I'm not going to be here for supper. I guess you know I'm going to meet Andy."

"Oh Cyn! I'm making this spaghetti especially for you. We've hardly seen you lately. Won't you please stay?"

"But Laura…"

"You're going to be leaving so soon. I really want to see a little of you before you go."

"I guess I could stay for supper and meet Andy afterwards. Can I do anything to help you with it?"

"Thanks. I can do it. It'll be ready soon."

"Okay." She didn't say that she'd been feeling guilty about spending all her time with Andy and neglecting Laura and Paul and Orion. "If I can't do anything to help you, I'll go up and see if Paul needs a hand."

"I'll call you both when it's ready…and thanks."

Cynthia went outside. Andy would wonder why she wasn't there, but the spaghetti smelled good, and she missed spending time with Laura. She could explain it all to Andy later.

When she walked around the corner of the house, she saw Paul up in the field, standing beside his truck. He had his saw on the ground in front of him. While she watched, he pulled the cord several times. When it started, he picked it up and stood there revving it. Cynthia could see he was nervous. She couldn't say anything because of the noise, but she smiled and waved. He nodded in acknowledgement.

Probably because she was there, he didn't hesitate any longer. He walked over to the limb and started to cut. Cynthia watched while he sliced off several rounds of wood. He seemed less nervous now that he was actually doing it. She waited until he had sawed his way some distance along the limb.

Then she began to carry the logs one by one to the back of the truck. After a while, Paul turned off the saw and started helping her. When she took a break and stood leaning against the tailgate, he stopped beside her.

"Don't work so hard, Cynthy. We don't have to get it all today."

"It's not that hard. I was just catching my breath."

"This is going to be nice firewood. We didn't use our fireplace much last winter, but this year I'm planning to get the chimney inspected before it gets cold. Maybe you'll be here for the holidays. I'm hoping your mom and dad will have Christmas with us."

"I don't know if I will be. I'm not sure where I'll be by then."

"You'll be on school vacation, and your school isn't very far from here. It should work out fine."

"That's just it. I'm having trouble making up my mind about whether to go back to school or not. It seems so pointless."

"You'll get over that. It's just the sophomore slump talking. You know it's important. I'm going to get back to work. Laura will be calling us to dinner any minute."

Cynthia followed him, and they carried down some more wood. When they were both near the truck again, she said, "Are you glad you went all the way through to graduation?"

"Sure. I wouldn't have been able to get my job without it. It's not a perfect job, but it's okay, and it's why we were able to have Orion and put a down payment on the house."

"Laura doesn't seem to mind that she didn't finish."

"She can go back if she wants to when Orion is a little older. Has she ever said she was sorry she quit?"

"Not to me she hasn't. Actually, she doesn't seem sorry at all. That's another thing that makes me wonder why I should go back. What I want is to get out in the real world and learn practical things, not ideas from books."

"You'll have plenty of time for that after you finish."

"That's what everybody says, but I'm awfully sick of it. I could take a few years off now and go back later. That's what I feel like doing." She didn't say any more, but she pictured travelling across the country with Andy. He hadn't ever been anywhere. They could have lots of adventures together. He said he couldn't do that, but she might be able to convince him. After all, she thought she had made him see how wrong it was to go into the army.

"Have you talked to your parents about taking time off?"

"Are you kidding?" She made a face. "They would have a fit if I even suggested it."

Paul thought for a minute, and then he said, "I remember how they were when Laura quit to get married. They didn't like it at all."

"Can you imagine what they'd say if I wanted to do the same thing and without even a good reason like getting married?"

"I guess you'd better not try it."

"But the problem is that I *don't want* to go back. I want to learn useful things for a change, things I can use in my daily life."

"Have you talked to Laura about all this?"

"I haven't had a chance yet, but I'm going to." She didn't say that she knew Laura would think she was against school and learning because she was spending too much time with Andy. But she was going to have to talk to Laura, and she didn't have all that many chances left.

They went back to throwing wood into the pickup until Laura called them. Then they grabbed the last few logs, put the saw on top of the load, and drove down to the house and the spaghetti.

Partway through dinner, Paul said, "Cynthia's wondering whether to go back to school or not."

Laura had a spoonful of food halfway to Orion's mouth. She stopped. "What?" She looked horrified.

Cynthia was annoyed. She hadn't planned on saying anything to Laura tonight. She wanted to hurry away after dinner in order to get up to the camp and Andy before dark. She said, "I just asked Paul if he was glad he graduated. I can't help wondering what's the point of all this studying. I never do anything real."

Laura gave Orion the spoonful of food. Then she said, "I thought you liked it there, Cynthia."

"It's okay. I'm just sick of being in school. I want to be out in the world *doing* something."

Laura relaxed a little. "Don't worry. It'll still be there when you get done." She gave Orion another bite. He loved spaghetti. "It's not that different to be out of school, honestly."

"Are you sorry you quit, Laura?"

"No, not at all." She looked over at Paul. "But Paul and I had things we wanted to do together. You don't…oh dear…" She looked at Paul again and didn't say any more.

There was an uncomfortable silence. Cynthia thought about how she wanted to be with Andy. But she couldn't say it, so she changed the subject. "Have you heard anything from Bob?"

"As a matter of fact, we did. I forgot. I'm sorry. He's been out there for quite a while now. He said to tell everybody, and particularly you, Cynthy. He says it's a fantastic scene, and he's so glad he made it. He hopes you don't regret not coming with him."

"When's he coming back?"

"He didn't say anything about that."

"I guess if I'd gone with him, I wouldn't have been able to go back to school, would I?"

No one answered her question.

Laura took a couple of bites for herself and one for Orion. "I hope you're not going to say anything to Mom and Dad. They would blame me for somehow talking you into wanting to quit."

"I'd tell them it was my idea, not yours."

"Mom would still blame me."

Cynthia said, "I'm sorry we got into this whole subject. I didn't mean to cause a major family problem. It was just an idea I had."

When she was walking up the hill to meet Andy, she realized she had been thinking that he was the one who wasn't thinking about the future, but she was just as guilty. Here she was, only weeks away from going back to school, wondering if she wanted to be there this year. She should have been thinking about it long before this. And she shouldn't tie it to what Andy was going to do. She had to figure out what was right for her.

CHAPTER 24

Nellie was picking corn when Phyllis came along.

"Oh, here you are, Gram. I been lookin all over for you."

"Well, you found me."

"Are we goin to have that corn for supper?"

"If I find enough that's ready, and I think I will."

"I hope there's a lot. It's so good."

Nellie walked through the patch. Most of the ripe ones were on the outside rows. "The coons ain't been in here yet. Maybe they're still goin after your dad's field corn. It grows faster."

"I been tyin Moxie on the back porch every night. They're scared of her."

"She won't fool 'em for long. They're too smart. They'll figure out she's on a line."

When Nellie had a dozen ears in her apron, they took them back to the porch and sat down, side by side on the steps to shuck them. They put the husks in a paper bag and the ears of corn in a bowl.

"Andy don't sleep no more, Gram. What's he doin? He's got to sleep, don't he?"

"What're you *talkin* about, Phyllis?"

"Well, this is what I mean. I got to wonderin what Andy was doin at night. His door is closed, so you might think he was in his room, but one time when I got up in the middle of the night to pee, I opened his door real slow and quiet, and he wasn't in there. His bed was made, like it is in the daytime."

"It might have just been the one time."

"Uh-uh, Gram. I did it a whole bunch of times to see. I didn't find him in there even once. He don't sleep there no more."

"Phyllis, you got to take all the corn silk off. Your dad won't like it if it gets stuck in his teeth."

"I know that. I'm goin to go over 'em all at the end. Tell me what you think about Andy. What does he do all night?"

"That's his business, honey. We don't need to know. He's goin to be leavin so soon."

Phyllis stopped working and sat there looking down the hill. Then she said, "Yeah, Gram, remember when me and Andy went to that funeral?"

"Yes, of course. You came home and told me about it."

"Didn't Andy tell you about it too?"

"No, he didn't. I heard it all from you." Nellie didn't say so, but she was disappointed that Andy hadn't talked to her. She was afraid it meant he knew what he was going to do, and even seeing the collapse of Gary Sensi's mother didn't change his mind.

"I been thinkin, Gram. That could happen to Andy."

Nellie nodded. Of course it could.

"And I bet Ma would go even crazier."

"Did Andy say anythin to you, Phyllis?"

"No, and I bet he didn't tell Ma or Pop about it either."

"I guess we'll just have to wait and see."

They were all done with the corn. Nellie stood up slowly.

"You could ask him what he's goin to do, Gram."

"Maybe…if I get the right chance." She looked down at the top of Phyllis's head. She obviously hadn't combed her hair today.

"I'm goin to get Moxie. She was takin a nap. She's probably ready to get up by now."

"Have you been practicin with the deer rifle? I ain't heard any shots."

Phyllis stood up. She looked off down the hill again and not at Nellie. "I been meanin to…but Moxie don't like how loud it is."

"You don't have to bring her with you."

"I know, Gram. I'll do it soon."

"You have to do the work if you want to be a good shot."

"I know, Gram. If I had somebody to do it with me, it wouldn't be so scary."

"You got to get over it, Phyllis. That's all."

"I'll try, Gram."

Nellie sighed. She picked up the bowl of corn. "Throw that bag of shucks in the garbage bin out by the garden, will you?"

"Okay, Gram."

Nellie went into the kitchen. Patty probably didn't need to worry about Phyllis learning to shoot. Phyllis wasn't like Andy or Nellie. *They* had practiced all the time. Nellie remembered how she wanted to be like Annie Oakley.

CHAPTER 25

They were sitting on opposite sides of the fire. The daylight was almost gone, but Andy could see Crystal's face plainly by the light of the fire and the candles they had stuck on the rocks around them.

She said, "And you're sure you're not mad at me? Something's been wrong for a while now."

"I know, but it ain't you."

"What *is* it then? Please tell me."

He sighed. "It's just something I can't get out of my head. I didn't want you to think I was stupid, so I wasn't goin to tell you about it."

Crystal came around the fire and sat down. The branches creaked under her as she sat close beside him. She put her arm around his neck and kissed him on the cheek. "I want to know what it is. Maybe I can help."

"I don't think so. You've been tellin me all summer how bad it was to go to Vietnam, and I wouldn't listen. I didn't want you to see how long it took me to get what you were sayin."

"But, Andy, what made you change your mind?"

So, then he had to tell her about the funeral, and how Gary's mother collapsed over the coffin, and how that made him see what could happen in his family if he got killed in Vietnam. "And I know you've been tellin me this all summer, and I didn't hear you, but I don't know what I can do about it anyhow."

She kissed him on the cheek again. "I'm so glad you saw it before you signed up. What are you going to do?"

"That's why I wasn't goin to tell you. I don't know."

"*I* don't know what to do either. I have been thinking I didn't want to go back to school. It would be like this summer never happened."

"What would you do instead?"

She kissed him again. "What if we went together?"

"Into the army?"

"No, silly, if I quit school, we could drive around and see the country. I've heard of people avoiding the draft by not having a regular address."

He broke a stick into little pieces and tossed them onto the fire one by one. He watched the fire flare a little each time. "What would we do for money?"

"We wouldn't need much. We could camp, like we've been doing. We'd just need money for gas and food. We could find jobs along the way."

"But winter's comin."

"We could go south. This is a big country."

He didn't like it. "I don't know. I just can't see myself runnin away like that." Why couldn't they leave him alone. He thought about Pop. He would say that Andy was living in this country, where past generations had gone to war to protect his freedoms, and now it was his turn, even if he didn't see the point of this particular fight. He felt hemmed in on every side by people who thought they knew what he ought to do, even if he didn't know himself.

Crystal said, "I could go back to school, and you could come down and hide out there."

"No. I ain't goin to do that. It wouldn't take 'em long to figure *that* out. If they catch me, they'll put me in jail."

"Maybe they just say that to scare you."

"I don't want to chance it. If I sign up and go, I might could figure out how to get out of it while I'm there."

"Not when they've already got you, and you have to do what they say. They could tell you to shoot women and children, and you'd have to do it."

"I don't think I would do something like that."

"But see, if you didn't do as you were told, they'd put you in jail for disobeying."

"Well, I don't know what the answer is then. I guess there ain't a good one."

"I know." She leaned behind him and dug under the blanket and pulled out the bag of weed. She smiled at him and started to roll a joint. "Maybe this will give us some ideas of what to do."

He almost said no, but then he thought about it. Once more

wouldn't hurt, and their time together was getting short. Maybe she was right and smoking a joint would give them some new ideas, and even if it didn't, they could have a nice night together.

CHAPTER 26

Nellie was so busy trying to get Aurora to stop squawking and flapping, that she didn't see Andy when he came around the back of the house.

"What're you doin to that chicken, Gram?"

"Oh, Andy, you startled me. I'm tryin to get her ready for the fair."

"But it ain't for two more days. How're you goin to keep her clean?"

"This is just practice. I want her to get used to havin a bath, so I can do a good job tomorrow when I groom her for real. She's too scared to calm down right now. She thinks I'm goin to drown her." She said all that while trying to keep Aurora from thrashing around and getting her head under the water. "I ain't puttin soap on her today. I'll be doin a lot more next time."

"Is she the only one you're goin to show?"

"There's two more, but they know how to take a bath. They won't give me this kinda trouble." She took Aurora out of the water and rolled her up in the towel. "And it don't matter so much. I'm takin the other two to keep her company. Aurora's the one who's goin to win us the ribbon. You'll see."

"Is Pop goin to drive you?"

"Your pop and Phyllis and I are goin down Thursday morning. Your mom has to work. If we take her car, she can have the pickup. Phyllis'll have to skip school. I expect we'll be down there most of the day."

"That sounds like fun."

"You want to come with us? The box for the chickens needs to ride on the back seat, but there's plenty of room. That car is big."

"I don't know," Andy said. He looked troubled about something.

"I'm goin to put some cabbage leaves in the box, instead of a water dish, so it won't make a mess. Don't you want to take your girlfriend to the fair? I could loan you some money, and you could treat her. I bet she'd like it. She has a car, don't she? Maybe you could go in her car, instead of goin with us."

Andy looked down at his feet and kicked some clods of grass, but he didn't answer.

Nellie said, "There's a big storm comin in tonight, but after that, it should clear off. It might be cold, but I don't think it'll frost. I hope not anyhow. I ain't ready for it. I still got too much out in the garden. But cold and clear is just right for a night at the fair with your sweetheart." She smiled at him.

He didn't smile back. He just looked more worried. "I don't know. I might not want her to see it. There's a awful lot of rowdy drunks at Tunbridge. She could get the idea that all country people act that way."

"She's been here for a while. She knows better by now."

"And anyways, I don't know what *I'm* goin to do. I got the letter from the draft board."

"Is *that* what that was? I saw it layin on the table."

"I'm supposed to go down and register next Monday, and if I don't, they say they'll come get me and put me in jail."

"Oh honey!" Aurora was still. She must have thought it was night, wrapped up in the towel the way she was.

"What can I do, Gram?"

"I don't know. What does your girlfriend say?"

"She doesn't think I ought to go, but she don't know how I can get out of it. I ain't like her college friends. When I try to ask her what I should do instead, she gets me even more mixed up. She says if I go to Vietnam, they'll tell me to kill women and children, and I'll do it."

"Does she really believe that?"

"I don't know." His face was contorted. "Maybe she's right. Maybe I would."

"I don't think so, Andy—not you."

"Thanks, Gram. I don't think so either, but I just don't know for sure."

"You need to talk to her some more so you can make a decision." She couldn't say anything else. Frank wouldn't like it.

Andy sighed. "I know I should. But we're both out of time. She's got to go back to school this weekend." He sighed again. "I don't think it'll help to talk to her. Would it be okay if I took another package of hamburg?"

"You do that, Andy. And good luck."

After Andy left, Nellie unrolled the towel and helped Aurora stand up. She shook herself and fluffed out her feathers, and then she stretched up as tall as she could, like she was standing on tiptoe. Nellie had been planning to clip her claws, but she didn't have the heart to wrap her in the towel again, so she let her go. She could do it tomorrow evening when Phyllis would be there to help.

She didn't want to think about Andy's problem. She had tried *not* to think about what he should do when he turned eighteen. And now the summer was over, and the noose was tightening around him, and she still didn't know what he should do. It upset her to think about it. She put it out of her mind. She had too much to do before the day at the fair.

CHAPTER 27

The whole time Andy was milking, he was thinking about his conversation with Gram. She *meant* to help him. He knew that. Still, she hadn't made him see what he ought to do. She was right that he needed to talk to Crystal, but he didn't see how that was going to help. Crystal already was sure she knew what he should do, and she didn't understand how his options were different from those of her college friends.

He walked up to the camp, feeling worried and depressed. His short-term plan was to thaw and cook the hamburg he got from Gram and, if Crystal showed up, he would wait for just the right moment before he tried to talk to her.

Maybe Crystal couldn't help him much, but they could still have a romantic night together. That was how he said it to himself, even though he knew what he was really thinking about was sex. The romance part was just a way to get there.

The weather had him worried too. Clouds were moving in, and the air felt heavy. Gram was right, like she always was. There was going to be a big storm tonight.

When he walked into the camp, Crystal was already there, trying to make a fire. She looked up. "Help! I can't get it to go. What am I doing wrong?"

He set down the hamburg and crouched beside her.

She said, "I can tell you've milked, because you smell like a cow."

He was embarrassed. He should have changed his clothes. He had been in too much of a hurry to get to the camp to talk to her. He moved away.

"Don't. I like it when you smell like a barn."

That embarrassed him even more. He tried to concentrate on the fire, and after rearranging the scraps of wood and kindling, the flames burst up.

Crystal clapped her hands and kissed him on the cheek.

He left her to put on some bigger sticks, while he went to the brook to fill the kettle with water. He planned to use the hot water to thaw the meat, so he could make them some hamburgs, although they had nothing to put on them, and they had eaten all the bread a while ago. This feeding themselves every day was turning out to be more complicated than he thought. Crystal didn't seem to notice.

When he came back with the kettle full of water, the fire was much bigger and burning brightly.

"The fire looks great," he said. "I hope we can protect it from the rain."

"It's not raining."

"It's goin to. There's a big storm comin in tonight."

"How do you know?"

"Gram said so."

"Maybe she's wrong."

"Gram always knows. It feels like it anyways."

She smiled a wicked smile. "We'll have to get under the covers and stay there until it's over."

His heart gave a lurch. It was exactly what he wanted to do. "That's fine with me," he said. "But it's still goin to put out the fire."

"We won't be cold, I promise." She was still smiling that smile.

"I got a idea of how to protect it."

He put the kettle on the fire, and it wasn't long before the water was boiling. He poured it over the package of hamburg. "Wait a minute until I start the hamburg cooking, and then I'll set it up." After the hot water had thawed most of the hamburg, he made it into patties and put them in the Dutch oven on the fire.

Then he got a flat stone from the edge of their clearing. It was so big that he couldn't lift it, but he managed to roll it toward the fire, like an irregular wheel. When he got it close enough, he asked Crystal to keep it from tipping over while he put a few rocks in place. That took some doing, and Crystal got impatient steadying the rock, but finally he had the supporting rocks set, and he was able to lower the big flat one into place, like a shed roof over their fire.

He had been watching the hamburgs cook while he arranged the stones. He took the pot off the fire as soon as his hands were free. "I hope you like your hamburgs well done."

"They smell really good. I wish we had some bread and catsup."

"Me too." Andy put some wood on the fire and set the pot beside their bed. He put the lid on the pot to keep the food warm and dry.

It started to rain while they were eating. They both moved back under the tarp roof. The fire hissed when drops hit it, but most of the rain was deflected.

"I told you it was goin to rain. My rock roof might could work."

"Your Gram is amazing. I wish I could predict the weather like that."

"She's lived on our farm since she was young. Maybe if she was some place else, she couldn't do it. She wouldn't know what signs to look for."

"It's very cool."

"She told me to ask you what you thought I ought to do. She said she couldn't give me the right advice, but you could." It wasn't much of an exaggeration.

"Me?"

"I don't know what to do."

"I don't know what *I* ought to do either."

"I thought you were going to go back to school this weekend."

"I've been wondering whether to go back or not."

"If you quit school, where would you go? Would you stay here?"

She snuggled closer to him where they sat under the tarp, even though it was getting quite hot, with the big, slanted rock reflecting the heat from the fire onto them. The rain was coming down harder now, drumming loudly on the tarp over their heads and making the fire pop and hiss.

"Look what a place you have made for us out of nothing. That's how I want to live. I want to stay here with you."

For just a second, he loved what she said. Then he thought about it. "But I won't be here."

She pulled away and looked into his face without saying anything.

"I got the letter from the draft board. I ain't got a choice. I got to report to them, or they'll come and get me. And that means jail."

"You're not seriously thinking about..."

"I don't see what else I can do. I've always known this was goin to happen. *You* knew it too."

"I knew we *talked* about it. I thought you said you weren't going to go to Vietnam, that you knew you couldn't do that."

"I know I don't want to..."

"But you *can't*. You know you can't!" She was bouncing up and down with excitement. "And it's not just about you. Think what it would do to your family. Think what it would do to me. How am I supposed to protest the war when I have a boyfriend who's killing people?"

"You ain't protestin the war."

"What?"

"I ain't seen you doin any protests."

"Oh," she said. "That's not true. Just because you haven't seen...well, it's because I've been spending all my time with you this summer, but it's important. I'm going to be doing more soon. You'll see."

"I won't be here to see. I already got the notice. I got to report to the draft board so they can see if they want me."

"See, there you go—leaving it up to them again."

"Crystal, don't be stupid! They will put me in jail if I don't show up. You know that. I was hopin to find a way out, but I haven't. I don't think there *is* one. I'm goin to have to go."

They were sitting farther apart now. Andy wanted to reach out and touch her, but he was afraid she wouldn't like it.

"Don't call me stupid! We should have talked about all of this a long time ago. Now it's too late. Of course, I know about the draft! I still believed you would change your mind and come down with me when I went back to school. We could have figured it out together. I have friends who know about the draft...maybe not in Vermont, but..."

He wondered whether there was a chance of changing the subject. Whatever happened was going to happen, and they probably couldn't stop it, no matter what she thought. But they still had a little time left to make love. The hippies all said, "Make love, not war." He didn't say that out loud either, but he was thinking it as he moved closer and put his arm around her.

"Don't," she said, and she twitched her shoulders to throw off his arm.

"I love you, Crystal."

"That's not true! If it was, you wouldn't sign up for the war. You know how I feel about it. If you sign up for the draft, I won't be your girlfriend any more."

"Oh," he said. He felt like he had been punched in the gut, and yet he'd known it right along, hadn't he? "We can still love each other," he said, even though it felt lame when he said it.

"I don't see how," she said. "If you're going to be a soldier and go to Vietnam, then it's over for us, and that's final."

"Don't say that, Crystal, please…" He reached toward her, and she sprang away. "Crystal, don't…"

She jumped up and ran out of the circle of firelight. The rain was pouring down. He knew she wouldn't get far in the dark and the wet, and when she came back, he would hold her and warm her, and they would make love, maybe for the last time. They had always known it would have to end.

He put some wood on the fire and sat there patiently, because he knew she would be back, and she would be cold and wet. He didn't think she knew enough about the woods at night to get herself to her sister's house, even though their camp was on the Robinson side of the hill.

Then, after a while, he wasn't so sure any more. He began to think she must be lost. He didn't want to leave his warm spot by the fire, but he pictured her shaking with cold and fear, and he knew he had to go and find her.

He spent the whole night looking. He would come back to the camp to put more wood on the fire and then go out again. He kept thinking of new directions to try. There wasn't any sense in doing anything about his clothes because they couldn't get any wetter.

The rain finally let up around daybreak. He left a little fire burning, just in case she might need it, and sick with cold and worry, he went down to get dry clothes and to milk.

CHAPTER 28

When he told her he was going to sign up for the war and in the same breath that he loved her, Cynthia jumped to her feet. She had just said that if he joined the army, she wouldn't be his girlfriend any more. So, what was he thinking? It didn't make sense. If he loved her, he wouldn't go to war.

When she stood up, she was out from under the tarp. The rain was pouring down and soaking her, but she couldn't get back under the tarp because Andy was there, reaching out toward her and saying he loved her. And she couldn't stay where she was, getting wetter by the minute.

She started to run, out of the circle of firelight, into the blackness of the night. She couldn't see a thing, and she couldn't hear anything either. The rain was making too much noise. She put her hands out in front of her and stumbled forward, hoping she was going toward the trail. She was sure Andy was right behind her, and she didn't want him to touch her, not now, not after what he had just told her. Everything she had believed about their love was a lie. They had had fights before, but this one was different. It was as though the scales had fallen off her eyes, and for the first time, she could see how it really was. He had only meant it to be a pastime for the summer, while he waited until he could ship out. She had changed all her plans because she believed him. She was a fool.

If she hadn't been completely overwhelmed by her thoughts, she never could have gotten to Laura and Paul's house, but somehow, stumbling and crying, only conscious that she needed to be always going downhill, she came out of the trees into the back field. She was on the edge of the field, near where she and Paul had picked up the wood. If she had gone at more of an angle, she might have missed the field altogether. She was grateful to whatever had guided her.

When she got to the house, she went in through the kitchen and climbed the back stairs. No one saw her, even though she could hear their voices not too far away. She got out of her soggy clothes and had a hot shower and got into bed without having to explain anything to Laura. In that, she was lucky again.

CHAPTER 29

As soon as he finished putting away the morning's milk and eating the breakfast Gram had kept warm for him, Andy went back to the camp.

The hard rain of last night was over. This morning everything sparkled, washed clean in the sunlight. Gram was right. It was going to be cold but clear—autumn weather for a few days, perfect for the Tunbridge Fair.

All the way up the hill he kept hoping Crystal would be there beside the fire. Or if she really didn't want to see him again, that there would be some evidence that she *had* been there. But there was nothing. He was sure she hadn't been back since he left.

The fire was burning low. He put on some sticks and sat down under the tarp. He could search the woods again, but he had already looked in every direction he could think of, and the rain had washed away any tracks she might have made.

The next thing he knew, he woke up, lying on the pine-bough bed under the tarp. The fire was out. The shadows had a midday look to them.

He still didn't know what his long-term plan could be. The only thing he was sure of was that he would have to dismantle the camp. He got up and started to work. While he scrubbed Gram's pots in the brook, he kept looking over his shoulder, hoping Crystal would appear behind him, laughing and glad to see him. After a while, he knew it wasn't going to happen.

At first, all he was clear about was what he *wouldn't* do. He couldn't go with Crystal to her school, and he couldn't go into the army. He wouldn't do what Crystal wanted him to do, and he wouldn't do what everyone else thought he ought to do. He wasn't going to be ordered around by anyone, no matter what Crystal thought. He would go his own way.

Slowly, as he worked to demolish their camp, his new idea came into focus. He always felt at home in the woods, so he would build on that. He would take a few essential things—some food, an ax, and a gun—and he would go straight north to Canada, staying out of sight in the woods until he got there. Everyone he knew would say he was a coward and a draft dodger, but he didn't care, and anyway, maybe he was.

Cheered by finally having a plan, he worked hard to make the spot look natural, as though there had never been a camp in that place. He made two piles—one of all the things he meant to carry with him, and a second pile of things, like Pop's big tarp, that he was going to return on Thursday when everyone was gone to the fair.

He didn't dare say goodbye, not even to Gram or Phyllis. They would worry too much. They might even try to stop him. He would have to leave secretly at night. If he made it to Canada, he would telephone them to tell them he was safe. He knew he could never go home again, but maybe they would come to Canada to visit him. It wasn't that much farther than Tunbridge, and they went there every year.

In the morning, they did the chores early. Andy helped load Ma's car. Ma had to work, but everyone else was going to the fair. Phyllis even got to take a day off school.

They put a blanket over the back seat and set the chickens' cage on top of it. Gram had put cabbage leaves on the bottom of the cage, in case the chickens were thirsty.

Andy was filled with tender sadness as he helped them get the chickens settled. He watched them all climb into the front seat and drive away. Soon he would have to leave himself. He would never see any of them again.

After they drove off, he spent the rest of the morning bringing down everything he had taken up to the camp. He put back Pop's tarp and Gram's kettle and hid his things in the woods below the house.

Then he hitchhiked into town and spent the little money he had on food to carry with him. He saved a few dollars for the phone call, but there wasn't any sense in taking money to Canada since they used different money there. He knew people could change one kind of money for another, but he didn't know how to do it.

His plan was set. Crystal was the only one who could have changed it. When he was alone at the house, he kept hoping she would come up the road, and later, when he hitchhiked into town, he kept looking for her little black car. He almost didn't want to catch a ride, because then he might miss her, but at the same time, he realized it was a hopeless dream and he needed to get on with his own life.

By the time everyone got home, he was ready to leave. They had so much to tell about the fair that no one noticed how he was feeling. He kept thinking he was leaving everything he had ever known.

CHAPTER 30

All day Wednesday Cynthia was sure she didn't want to see Andy. She gathered her things together to pack in her car for school. In the afternoon, she went to the laundromat, and on the way home, she saw a hitchhiker. She slowed down with her heart beating fast, but when she got close, she saw it wasn't Andy after all, and she sped up again, leaving the hitchhiker looking confused.

That night after supper, she found Laura sitting in front of the television, breast-feeding Orion while she watched the news.

"Here you are, Laura," she said. "Where's Paul?"

Laura looked up. "He's outside doing something. I don't know what. Come and sit down. I saw you were packing up your car. What are your plans?"

"I'm sorry, Laura. I should have told you sooner. I'm going to leave on Friday, or Saturday morning at the latest. I'm going back to school. I hate to leave. It has been a wonderful summer."

"It has been for me too. I've loved having you here. The one thing I'm sad about is that we didn't get down to see Papa when he got home from the hospital. I meant us to drive down there. We might have even gotten Paul to go with us. We should have planned better."

"I know. We could have worked it in if we'd tried. I guess they're doing okay, now that he's home."

"That's what Mom says." Laura sat Orion up for a minute to change sides. He was so groggy that his eyes wouldn't focus. Laura patted him on the back and then laid him down on the other side. "I'm so glad you've decided to go back to school, Cyn."

Cynthia sat near the television set. "Yes, well, my idea of taking a year off just didn't work out, so I guess I have to go back."

"What's Andy going to do?"

Cynthia had a struggle to stay calm. "He's going into the army. He meant to do it all along, only that's not what he told me. I'm sure they'll send him straight off to Vietnam."

Just as she said it, a battle story came on the news. There were explosions and shouts, and men carrying stretchers. She burst into tears. Both of them watched without talking, until the news shifted to another story.

"I told him if he went to war, it was all over with us."

Laura sighed. "I always said he was too different...his background... but I know you cared..."

"Yes, I did..." She stopped to get more control of her voice. "That was before I knew that he wasn't listening to anything I told him. He was just pretending to hear me." She started to choke up again. "I feel betrayed. He was so deceptive."

"I only saw him a couple of times, but he didn't strike me as being deceptive at all...naïve, maybe." She thought for a minute. "But I never thought he would think the way *we* did."

"Yes, I know."

"Did you say goodbye to each other already?"

"No. We had a fight, and I left without saying anything."

"And you're going to leave it like that?"

"I don't know. I guess so."

"Look, Cyn, I always thought it was a mistake, but I know you really cared for him. Why don't you try to part on good terms and then wait and see if at the end of the year, you still have feelings for him...well, you could get back in touch."

"Suppose he gets killed? It's very likely if he's sent to Vietnam."

"That's another good reason to part on better terms. I don't say you should write to him or anything, but I do think you should give yourself some room, in case you find you can't forget him. You might feel differently about him when he comes home. By then he might have realized that you were right about the war."

Cynthia kept thinking about what Laura said. Maybe Laura's words convinced her, or maybe it was the ache in her heart that made her want to see him and talk to him one last time. On Thursday she spent hours in Laura's garden, watching the woods above, hoping he would come down if he saw her there. He had done it before.

When he didn't come, she decided to go over to the Keyes farm at milking time. But she couldn't get away. Laura was planning a special farewell dinner, and she needed Cynthia's help watching Orion. Then she decided to go up to their camp before dark to see if he was there. She thought he would be, but that was a failure too. By the time the dinner was over and cleaned up, it was too close to dark. She tried not to be annoyed with Laura, who told her to say goodbye to him and then made it impossible to do.

It was early Friday morning before she had a good chance to get away. She went up the back field and into the woods, full of excitement and with a fast-beating heart.

The camp was gone. She stood there, looking around. The sticks and pine boughs that had made their bed, and the shelter above it, weren't there. The big rock had been lowered onto the firepit. It looked like an ordinary pile of rocks. She couldn't imagine how he had done all that by himself.

The only thing that showed that their camp had been in that place was a neat pile of Laura's candles on a rock. It was a rude sign, a middle finger raised against her.

She was too surprised and angry even to cry. She picked up the candles and left. Back at Laura's, she put the candles in the cupboard, said goodbye to Laura and Orion, and left for school. It was over.

CHAPTER 31

Friday morning Nellie was just clearing away the breakfast dishes when Frank came storming in. "Where the hell is Andy at?" he said from the doorway.

"I ain't seen him yet. He must be milkin. I've got his food put by on the back of the stove. He'll be in to get it."

"Well, he ain't in the barn, and he ain't done the milkin. Rosie's bellowin her head off, and her bag's full."

Nellie said, "I don't know where he could be if he ain't down there."

Just then Phyllis came in. She was wearing her school clothes.

"Is Andy upstairs?"

"I don't think so."

"Maybe he overslept. He ain't done the milkin like he always does."

Phyllis ran upstairs. In a few minutes she was back. "He ain't in his room, and it looks all neat in there, like he didn't sleep in his bed. Are you sure he ain't in the barn?"

They were standing around looking puzzled when Patty came in ready to go to work. "What's goin on?" she said.

Nellie stopped putting dishes in the sink and dried her hands on the dish towel.

Phyllis left the room and came back a few minutes later. "His deer rifle's there, but his shotgun is gone." she said. "It ain't in the gun cabinet."

"I don't understand," Patty said. "What're you talkin about?"

Phyllis said, "We can't find Andy, and his shotgun is gone from the gun cabinet."

"But it ain't even deer season." Patty said. "What could it mean? He wouldn't..." She sat down in the nearest chair and looked up at Frank with fear in her face.

"Now, Patty, it's too soon to jump to conclusions."

Phyllis said, "He was actin kinda weird last night. What did you think, Gram?"

"I didn't notice particularly, but I was busy gettin dinner when we got home. I wish I'd paid more attention."

Phyllis said, "He hugged me and kissed me and said I should take care of everybody. I didn't know what it was about. It made me feel funny."

Patty moaned. "Why would he…" Then she sat up straighter in her chair. "I bet it has somethin to do with that hippie girl…oh, I'm goin to call in sick today. I can't go to work until I know Andy's okay."

"I'm not goin to school either."

"But, Phyllis, that'll be two days in a row…"

"I don't care. You can't expect me to go when Andy could be in trouble…or worse…"

Frank said, "All right. We've got to find him. I'm goin to look in the barn again, and, Phyllis, you need to milk Rosie right away."

"But, Pop, I want to look for Andy. Maybe he's up in the woods."

"You can look there after you milk."

"I don't think it's fair. I do a lot of work around here."

"And you're goin to do even more until Andy comes back. You're goin to have his chores to do too."

"Aw, Pop…"

"Get goin."

When everyone left the room, Nellie opened the cupboard where she kept the pots and pans. The kettle she had loaned to Andy was back in its place, but the Dutch oven wasn't with it.

She went upstairs to his room. His bed was neatly made, but the blanket was missing. She picked up the corner of the mattress, and there was the letter from the draft board.

Those were all clues, but they didn't really add up. Nellie wished he had left them a note. She guessed he must have gone with the hippie girl, and he didn't want them to know.

She thought about it for a while, and then she went and got the cash box they kept for milk sales. She looked through the milk money until she found a check from the girl's sister at the old Robinson farm. There was a name and address and even a phone number on the check.

She didn't make the call until it was almost noon. She felt stupid saying they couldn't find Andy, like he was an object they had misplaced. But the woman named Laura was nice about it, even though she wasn't much help. She said her sister Cynthia had left a few hours ago for school. That name didn't sound quite right to Nellie, but she wasn't sure enough to say anything about it. Laura didn't think Andy went with her, but she could be wrong. Laura promised to call her sister as soon as she arrived at her school. It would be several hours before she could get her.

Nellie made sure she stayed near the phone, but when the call finally came, it wasn't good news. Laura said Andy had not gone with her sister after all, and her sister had no idea where he could be. All they could do was let each other know if they heard anything.

Saturday was a terrible day. Nellie and Patty spent most of it sitting at the kitchen table, drinking cup after cup of tea and waiting for the telephone to ring. The only time it rang was when Phyllis called collect from the fair to see if they had heard anything, but they hadn't. Frank spent a lot of time in the woods and came back with nothing to report. Everyone was jumpy and restless, but no one could do any work.

On Sunday Nellie and Frank had to go back to Tunbridge to pick up the chickens. When Phyllis got home on Saturday she told them that there were several blue ribbons on the chickens' cage, but Nellie didn't care very much. They hurried to the fair and back home again as fast as they could, thinking only that they wanted to be near the phone, just in case.

CHAPTER 32

Andy walked to the edge of the woods. It was almost dark. He was pretty sure it was Sunday night, and that meant everyone at home had been worrying about him for three days. He longed to call them, to hear their voices and to let them know where he was, but it was too soon. He was near Troy, so he ought to be on the border tomorrow. He would call them just before he crossed into Canada.

Now that he was so close, he was much less worried about getting caught by the draft board. He thought he would be worrying a lot less, but he found he was as anxious as ever. He was just worrying about other things. Was he going to find anyone in Quebec who spoke English? What was he going to do for food? He had hardly eaten anything but hot dogs for days, and he was about to run out of them. He wished he'd asked Gram where the Maxim boy crossed the border, and where he was now. If he could find him, maybe he would help.

He was leaving behind everything he cared about, everything he knew. Every time he thought of anything, it was something from his old life and old self that was over. Maybe he should have gone with Crystal, but he knew that didn't make any sense. It wouldn't have taken them very long to figure out where he was. This was the only way that had a chance of working, since he knew he didn't want to go to Vietnam and kill people. He had to give up everything he cared about, maybe even Crystal.

He had nothing but what he was carrying with him. He wished he hadn't brought the Dutch oven. It was so heavy, and he hadn't used it. He couldn't leave it in the woods, because it came from home, and Gram gave it to him. He put it in the bottom of his pack. He took his shotgun apart and wrapped the pieces in his clothes and put them in the pack.

He had four hot dogs left. He could eat them during the night as he walked. He hadn't been hungry. Most of the time, the worry and the sadness gave him a stomach ache. The only thing to do was to keep walking. The emptiness that he felt wasn't so bad as long as he kept moving.

He rolled up the blanket and tied it under the pack. He slung the pack over his shoulders and started to walk just inside the woods. As it got later, there were fewer cars. He moved out to the edge of the road where it was easier walking.

CHAPTER 33

Nellie was just beginning to pick up the breakfast dishes when the phone rang. Frank was still at the table.

"Maybe that's about Andy," she said, as she went to answer it. Out the window she could see Patty and Phyllis driving down the hill. It was too late to call them back.

The operator said there was a collect call from Andy and would she accept the charges. "Frank," she said. "It's Andy himself." And into the phone she said, "Yes. We'll accept the charges."

"Gram? It's me."

"Oh, Andy, are you all right? Where are you?"

Frank was standing up now, looking at her.

"I'm right on the border to Canada. I'm okay."

"Oh honey, how did you get there?"

"I walked. I didn't dare call you before this."

Frank was motioning to her to give him the phone, but she wanted to hear more from Andy. "Have you had enough to eat?"

"I've been eatin hot dogs the whole way. And once I got some field corn and cooked it. I'm not that hungry."

"Honey, I'm goin to give the phone to your pop." She handed the phone to Frank, but she stood close to him, and he tilted the phone so she could hear what Andy said.

"Hello, Andy. This is Pop. What're you goin to do in Canada?"

"I hope I can find somethin, Pop."

"You'll have to, won't you? You can't come back."

"I know that. Is Ma there? I'd like to say hello to her and Phyllis."

"I can tell 'em you said so. Ma's at work, and Phyllis went to school. They both missed Friday because they were worried about you."

"I'm sorry, Pop. I couldn't call until I got to the border."

"You're goin to go through with this then?"

"I ain't got a choice, Pop. I don't feel right about this war. I don't want to kill people for no reason. Besides, it's too late now."

"That makes you a draft dodger. You look like a coward."

"I'm sorry, Pop. I know this ain't what you wanted me to do."

"It sure ain't. I don't know how you came to such a screwed-up way of thinkin."

Frank was getting more and more stirred up. Nellie snatched the phone away from him. "Andy," she said. "Will you let us know where you get to and how you're doin?"

"As soon as I know, Gram. If I can't call, I'll write to you. Maybe you can come visit me sometime. It ain't that far."

"Oh honey, we can do that. You just take care of yourself now." And then he was gone.

When Patty and Phyllis got home, Nellie told them everything Andy said. They all agreed they were glad he was all right, and the three women were even glad he wasn't going to be a soldier. But Frank got upset and had to go out onto the porch to calm down.

CHAPTER 34

When Cynthia answered the dorm telephone at the end of the hall, Laura said, "Oh, Cynthy, I'm glad I got you."

"Laura? I've been answering the phone nonstop, hoping you'd call. Have you heard anything about Andy?"

"Yes. I just talked to his grandmother."

"Is he all right?"

"He is! He called them this morning. He was on the border, about to cross into Canada."

"Canada?"

"It took him three days to get there. He walked through the woods."

"That sounds like Andy."

"I thought he was going to enlist."

"I know. I thought so too."

"He heard what you said about the war, Cynthy. You must have said something that convinced him."

"I guess so. I don't know what it was though. He didn't say anything about Canada the last time I saw him. It's a complete surprise to me."

"He can't come back. They'd arrest him."

"I know. Poor Andy. That farm was the center of his life. He didn't want to be anywhere else."

"I asked his grandmother what he was going to do now, but she didn't know."

"I wonder if they're mad at me for talking him out of joining the army."

"She didn't sound mad. She sounded relieved."

"Andy's father was the hawk. I know his mother didn't want him to go."

"She's probably glad he went to Canada. What about you?"

"I'll have to think about it. It hasn't sunk in yet. I wish he'd told me that's what he was thinking of doing."

"Maybe he would have, if you'd talked to him again."

"Yes, maybe…but I think he didn't want anybody telling him what to do."

"And what about school? Are you at all glad to be back?"

"Oh, I don't know…by the end of the summer, I was feeling that school was pointless, and I guess that hasn't changed. But the truth is that I don't really feel like I *am* back. I've been thinking about Andy and staying by the phone so I wouldn't miss your call. I haven't seen anybody, and my classes don't start until tomorrow. Now that I know Andy's okay, I'll have to think about what *I'm* doing."

After she hung up, she went back to her room and sat on the bed to try to absorb what she'd heard. Andy had listened to her when she said the war was wrong. He'd listened and then made up his own mind what to do about it. That was the important thing. She hoped his parents didn't blame her for her part in it. She felt bad enough already. He was in a foreign country, and he couldn't go home.

She got dressed and went to the dining hall for some lunch. There was a lot of activity on campus. Everyone was moving in and saying hello to old friends. She didn't see anybody she wanted to talk to. What could she say when someone asked her about her summer? How could she explain it?

She went to the bookstore and bought some of the books she needed for her English courses. They were going to read Moby Dick in American Literature. She was excited about that.

Over the next few days, she began to sort out how she felt. Andy *had* listened to her, but she saw that she hadn't listened to him. She thought she already knew what he was thinking. She only listened when he was telling her something practical, like how to make a fire. She believed he was taking his ideas about the war from other people, and at first, he was. But he heard what she said that contradicted what he had thought, and he began to think it through. That was what was important. He sorted it out for himself.

She wished she could tell him how impressed she was by that, and how sorry she was that they hadn't talked more, and how she wished she had listened to him the way he had listened to her. She had been too sure that she knew the answer.

Gradually, she settled into the routine of school, even while still thinking about how she had lost Andy. There was an emptiness, a blankness. Everything she had thought about during the summer was gone.

Then she remembered that the last thing she said to him was that if he signed up to be a soldier and go to Vietnam, she wouldn't be his girlfriend any more. She had said it in anger and hadn't thought of it since. Did he hear that too? He chose not to enlist. He gave up everything else in his life, but it was possible that he didn't mean to give her up, that by going to Canada, he was leaving the door open for her to come find him, only she didn't know how.

Then she got a call from Laura.

"Cynthy, I'm glad I caught you. This letter came in today's mail. It's addressed to 'Crystal at the Robinson Farm.' That's you, isn't it? Didn't Andy call you Crystal?"

"Yes, I told you that."

"Do you want me to open it and read it to you?"

"Oh, Laura, thanks, but I think I want to read it first. I'll tell you what's in it. Put it in an envelope and send it to me, will you? Send it as soon as you can, okay?"

"All right, Cyn, but I want to know what he says."

"I'll call you when I get it. Thanks, Laura."

For the next three days, Cynthia checked her mailbox over and over. When the letter finally got there, she took it back to her dorm room so she could read it in private. Her hands were shaking as she opened it.

Dear Crystal,

I hope I can figure out how to get this letter to you. If you are reading it then you got it. I hope you can read my writing okay. My penmanship is not the greatest.

You probably know this already. I am in Canada. I walked through the woods so I wouldn't get caught and crossed the border at North Troy. No one tried to stop me. All the time I was walking I was thinking about you and the last time I saw you. When you ran off in the night and the rain. Did you get home okay? I looked for you all that night but I couldn't find you. Are you back at school? Are you glad to be there?

When I crossed the border, I walked for a few miles and came to a town called Mansonville. It had a little store. I didn't have any money so I sat down on the porch to figure out what to do. A woman came along and started talking to me. Luckily she spoke English. When she heard that I was a draft dodger she took me to her house and gave me some breakfast. I've been here ever since. She has 3 little boys and she's very glad they don't have to face the draft like I did. I'm lucky she came along. She says there's a new ski area in town started by some local people and she thinks I have a good chance of getting a job with them. She knows them. She's going to put in a good word for me. I know how to build trails through the woods and she says they want more trails and are hiring local people to make them.

It looks a lot like home around here. This house is right on the Missisquoi River that goes through Vermont too. Some guys in my school used to work at the Stowe ski resort on their winter vacation. The mountain here is even called Owl's Head like the one in Vermont. If they give me a job I will stay right here near the border. It's not that far from West Severance.

Will you write to me, Crystal, and tell me how you are? Mrs. Atwell, where I'm staying, says you can write to me at her address. I'm putting it at the bottom of the letter. I hope you are still my girlfriend. I didn't join the Army. I still love you so much.

Love, Andy

Andy Keyes
c/o Marion Atwell
20 Rue Mill
Mansonville, Quebec, Canada

When Cynthia got to the end of the letter, she went back to the beginning and read it again. Her first thought was relief that he was okay. Then she thought about herself. She could write to him. She would have to tell him that her name was really Cynthia, so he could put it in the address. But it wasn't over, unless she wanted it to be, and these few weeks back at school had shown her that she didn't want it to be over.

She called Laura and told her what Andy said about himself, leaving out the part where he said he still loved her.

"Are you going to write to him?"

"Yes. He said I could send a letter by way of the woman whose house he's staying in."

"Do you want me to call his grandmother?"

"No. You don't need to. I'm sure he has written to them too."

"Well, Cynthy, what does this mean for you?"

"I'm not sure yet, but I'm glad it's not over. I'll see how it goes. Maybe when I'm at your house at Christmas, I'll go up and see him in Canada. I think I'd like to do that."

ALSO BY RUTH PORTER

Unexpected Grace

Ordinary Magic

The Simple Life

Father to Daughter:
The Family Letters of Maxwell Perkins

Ruth Porter was born in New York City and grew up in Alliance, Ohio, where her father was a doctor. She graduated from Laurel School in Cleveland, and from St. John's College in Annapolis, Maryland. She did a year of secretarial school in Boston and then got married to Bill Porter. In 1964, they went to Vermont, to Clarendon Springs, near Rutland. After eight years they moved to a hill farm in Adamant, near Montpelier, where Ruth has lived ever since. Bill died in April, 2022.

Ruth raised four children and took care of the farm. (One of the children said that she and Bill learned everything they knew about farming from books, and most of those books were novels.) They had varying numbers of sheep, cows, pigs and chickens, and a big garden. Altogether, they raised most of their food.

Ruth spent her whole life reading and writing, but she began working on serious fiction during those hectic years. She has published four novels, as well as a book about her grandfather, Maxwell Perkins, one of America's most widely respected editors. Bill and Ruth started the publishing company, Bar Nothing Books, in 2005.

For more information about Ruth Porter and Bar Nothing Books go to: www.ruthkingporter.com and www.barnothingbooks.com.

www.ingramcontent.com/pod-product-compliance
Lightning Source LLC
Chambersburg PA
CBHW070355200726
48294CB00003B/931